The LAST
GIFT

The LAST GIFT

By

GARY E. PARKER

Chariot Victor Publishing
A Division of Cook Communications

Chariot Victor Publishing
A division of Cook Communications, Colorado Springs,
Colorado 80918
Cook Communications, Paris, Ontario
Kingsway Communications, Eastbourne, England

This book is a work of fiction. Any resemblance to actual
events or locales or persons,
living or dead, is purely coincidental.

Editor: Greg Clouse
Cover & Interior Design: Paul Segsworth
Cover Photo: Hellstrom Studios

1 2 3 4 5 6 7 8 9 10 Printing / Year 03 02 01 00 99

Library of Congress Cataloging-in-Publication Data
Parker, Gary E.
    The last gift/by Gary E. Parker
        p.   cm.
    ISBN   1-56476-779-5
    I.   Title
PS3566.A6784L37   1999   99-27375
813'.54--dc21   CIP

This book is dedicated to my mom and dad.
Though life was never easy for them, they
blessed me and my brother and two sisters in ways
we can never name. For those unspeakable gifts,
I am grateful.

CONTENTS

Chapter *1*

HOME

The snow started to fall just after 10 A.M. that frigid winter day, the day just prior to Christmas. For the first half-hour it drifted down slowly, as gentle as a swan's feathers. But then it turned thicker and heavier and bits of sleet mixed in with it to form a sharp sheet of chilling ice. By noon at least four inches of cold white, whipped about by a swirling wind, had piled up in drifts and stacks on the roads that snaked in and out of the mountains around Brevard, North Carolina.

At twenty minutes past twelve, a chocolate brown four-wheel-drive utility vehicle turned right and plowed up the snow-covered gravel road that fronted the now-empty homestead of the Jubal Laws family. Its engine purring through the blustery wind, the four-wheeler swerved left, then right, then left again. About four hundred feet off the main highway, the machine ground to a halt on the chimney side of a two-story, white frame house, and the door on the driver's side of the vehicle popped open. A second later a woman in gray slacks, white turtleneck sweater, wool coat, and black boots climbed out, gingerly placing down one boot at a time on the snowy driveway.

Pulling her hat, a battered-looking wool piece the color of her slacks, down over her ears, the woman exhaled a big draught of steamy breath, threw her head back, and gazed up for several seconds into the dark, gray sky. For a moment, it looked like she started to stick out her tongue to lick up some of the snow falling around her face. But then, as if suddenly expecting an asteroid or some other extraterrestrial object to come crashing through the clouds, the woman dropped her head, pulled her hat down tighter, and reached back into the four-wheeler. When she emerged from the vehicle again she held a small brown and white dog in her arms.

Clutching the dog, a toy collie, to her chest, she stood up straight and turned toward the house sitting thirty feet away. The frigid wind snapped across her face and she paused for a second to get her balance. The collie, obviously distressed by the cold, snuggled deep into her wool coat, burying his wet nose under her right arm. She kissed him on the head.

"Cheer up, Boo," she said, talking to herself as much as to him. "You're such a baby. It could be worse. We could be naked on a glacier at the North Pole."

Boo buried his head even further under her arm, obviously not sure if that would be worse or not. Given the circumstances, the woman tended to agree with him. Not even her vivid imagination could see anything any worse. Blowing a puff of white breath into the fury of the storm, she steeled herself and walked toward the house, her head low, her shoulders slumped. Usually, she loved snows like this one, loved the blanket of white it wrapped around the earth, the silence it coaxed from the world as it fell. In similar situations in the past, she had reveled in such wintry blasts—fixing snow cream, chugging down steaming cups of hot chocolate, and finding excuses to heave snowballs at anyone so unfortunate as to end up within range of her puny throwing arm.

But not this year—the year she turned forty and her mama died. This year the snow seemed brittle as it fell, hard like chunks of ice chipped from a block of glassy cold, chipped with a sharp pick and now lying jagged on the ground. The snow crunched under her boots as she stomped up the driveway and onto the wraparound wood porch that fronted her childhood home.

With a shiver, the woman unlocked the door, stepped inside, and flipped on an overhead light. The house was as quiet as the inside of a buried coffin. Only the sound of Boo's cowardly whining broke the silence. She dropped Boo to the floor and he nudged up against her legs, his slender body quivering. The woman shook her head disapprovingly. "Your name fits you, Boo," she said, nudging him away. "You think your own shadow is a ghost."

Her legs free of the dog, she closed the door, walked five steps farther into the house, and stopped. A huge room opened up before her, a cavernous space containing a dining room straight ahead, a den with a stone fireplace to her left, and a kitchen complete with a solid mahogany chopping block and handmade oak cabinets to her right. The stone in the fireplace, hauled by hand out of the Tanahoe Creek less than a half mile from the house, reached all the way up to a twenty-foot-high ceiling that overarched the entire space where she stood.

A mixture of familiar smells assaulted her nose as she looked over the room, including the aroma of eighty-two-year-old wood (cut and placed by her grandfather who had built the house at the turn of the century) and the smoky smell of years and years of warm fires burned in the fireplace. She wrinkled her nose, then took a step closer to the hearth. The popping and crackling of those fires had sung her to sleep over and over and over again in the eighteen years she had lived here.

For several more seconds, the woman let her eyes wander about. Over the fireplace mantel hung a huge family portrait—the last one taken. Her daddy and mama, Jubal and Catherine Laws, stood in the back. In the front—flanking her—posed her brothers Colin and Cory. And right smack in the middle she, Christina Catherine, sat on a chair with a smile on her face as wide as a coat hanger.

Shaking her head as if to clear from it something unpleasant, Christina glanced away from the portrait. To the left of it she saw a Christmas tree, a mountain spruce at least fourteen feet high and fully decorated with bright gold ribbons, solid white lights, and a whole slew of multi-colored ornaments. Though a stack of presents lay under the tree, the result of her sisters-in-law who always mailed most of their packages early for her mama to make ready, Christina felt no joy in seeing them. The idea of sharing gifts this year made her sad and somehow angry. For an instant she wondered when her mama had put up the tree, but then she knew the answer—sometime between the time she last saw her and the day of her sudden death.

Feeling slightly nauseous, Christina placed a hand on her stomach and looked up at the top of the tree. The final ornament, a ten-inch-high clear glass star that always crowned the tree, wasn't yet in place. That event would take place tonight, the last thing before the Bible reading.

She shoved aside the thought and let her eyes travel past the fireplace to a thick all-wood eating bar—the only thing separating the den from the kitchen—which wrapped itself around the chopping block and sink area. From the kitchen Christina sucked in a whiff of the other predominant smell of her childhood home—the tantalizing scent of baked bread. No matter how much time passed between her trips back home, she always knew the smell of bread would greet her when she returned. That smell seemed to have baked into the open oak beams that hung over her head and the hardwood floors that were getting wet from the melting snow dripping off her boots. She pulled off her hat, hanging it on a hook by the back door.

As she expected, she was the first one home. She was first in almost everything in her family of three siblings. Firstborn, first to go to college, first to marry, first, and for that matter, only, to leave their spouse. Her two brothers, Colin and Cory (her mama had a thing for "C's" since her full name was Catherine Cornelia), beat her in only one milestone. They both gave her mother grandchildren— Colin and his wife Beth combining to produce three and Cory and Sue Ann going them one better with four. It wasn't that Christina and her husband Bud hadn't done their best to beat them in the child-birthing contest. But four straight miscarriages made that contest one she had no chance to win. After she lost the fourth child in the fourth month of pregnancy, she and Bud decided to give up the effort. Pain tended to do that, she and Bud had decided—you hurt long enough and deeply enough and you'll definitely give up.

Leaving her overcoat hanging beside the scarf, Christina turned and tromped to the fireplace, Boo on her heels. She wanted to get a fire blazing before her brothers and their families arrived. Given her mindset, the last thing she needed was a bunch of nieces and nephews moaning and griping about a cold house.

Though she didn't like to admit it, Christina actually resented her brothers, their pleasant wives, and perfect children. They looked like the proverbial All-American families—all spit-shined, freckle-nosed, and overly content. Maybe that's why she didn't feel close to her siblings any longer. She didn't fit into that perfect picture.

At the fireplace now, she looked over the mantel but found no matches. Though she wasn't a smoker, she instinctively checked the pockets of her slacks. No matches there either. Boo nudged at her shins and she bent down to stroke him behind the ears.

"You cold, boy?" she asked.

Boo whined.

"Yeah, me too."

For several seconds she remained still, feeling totally out of place.

For the first time in her life, she didn't want to be home for Christmas. In fact, she admitted to herself, she felt awkward, like a stout woman at a supermodel convention. And she knew why. She was about to divorce her husband Bud and neither Cory nor Colin nor Beth nor Sue Ann knew what to say to her. And she felt the same way about them. Just as they couldn't speak her language, neither did she any longer know how to converse in theirs.

Not that she hadn't tried over the years. But, in spite of her best efforts, she found it impossible to speak honestly and graciously at the same time, to feel pleased that they had such wonderful marriages and had so successfully fulfilled the divine command to "be fruitful and multiply" while she had failed so miserably at both. Almost every time she saw one of their children, her first reaction was to grit her teeth. Why hadn't God given her body the capacity to bring healthy children to birth? What made her so unworthy to mother a baby?

Her brothers and their wives had conceived and delivered seven such babies into the world—four girls and three boys. And every one of them sported hair the color of beach sand and eyes the color of the sky at high noon on a clear day.

Yes, she and her brothers had grown apart over the years, for a variety of reasons. Their lives had careened away from each other, bounced this way and that, the phone calls getting less and less frequent, the excuses for not visiting each other easier and easier to make.

Christina sat down on the fireplace hearth and rubbed Boo behind the ears, her sagging mood pulling hard at her throat. Things hadn't always been so bad between her and her brothers. As children, they had slept in the same bed on Christmas Eve, their excitement seeming to multiply exponentially by the added company. Snuggling down under the covers, they waited with bright eyes and pounding hearts for Santa Claus to come, trying with all their childlike strength to stay awake until he did. But they always fell asleep, Colin and Cory on either side of her like in the portrait over the fireplace, their soft breathing a steady reminder of her place in a well-oiled system of order and peace.

It had been a long time since the days when she slept with her brothers on Christmas Eve. Now, they did well to meet more than once a year. Even their gatherings at Christmas seemed little more than perfunctory to her, reluctant meetings that only the most optimistic would dare call a celebration.

Make no mistake about it, either. They were meeting reluctantly that year. No one really wanted to come. Why should they? Both her mama and daddy were dead. Her daddy had been gone a long time, one of one hundred and twelve people who perished when a plane crashed into a blue-misted mountain outside Asheville twenty-nine years ago.

Christina stood and stared again at the portrait over the fireplace. The accident had occurred two months after the picture was taken—on a Saturday, three days before Christmas. The man in that portrait—a man with a thick mane of black hair and a chin that looked like God had chiseled it out of a granite quarry—had ended up scattered out in a million bits and pieces among the mountain laurels and maples that flourished in the Smoky Mountain air of the Appalachian Mountains.

The funeral was a blur to her, a fog of impenetrable memories. The only thing she vividly remembered was the preacher saying that if Daddy Jubal couldn't be with his wife and kids, he would just as soon be where he was, a part of the soil and soul of the Smokies that he loved so much. She remembered that phrase, "the soil and soul of the Smokies." And though she knew it was true about her daddy loving the mountains and in spite of the fact that she liked the way the preacher's words sounded when he said it, the phrase had offered her little consolation at the time. After all, she was only eleven, the elder sister of Cory, five, and Colin, four, a young girl with heavy responsibility and no daddy to hug when it all became too much to bear. They buried what they found of her daddy between two huge oaks that topped the ridge about two hundred yards out and up an incline that ran beyond the back door of the Laws' house.

Over the years, Christina had pretty much gotten accustomed to her daddy's absence. Not that it had been easy. But time and other things to worry about tend to push the most distant grief into the background. And no doubt about it, she did have more recent sorrows to keep her thoughts occupied. But Christmas always brought back to her the joyous memories of Jubal Basden Laws.

Leaving the fireplace, Christina shook her shoulders and stepped to her daddy's recliner, still sitting in the same spot it had occupied since the day of his death, barely ten feet away from the massive stone hearth. It looked as if it expected her daddy to come in any moment and plop down after a strong day's work. As the eldest child by six years and so the only one who could really remember him, she knew that the empty recliner meant more to her than to Cory and Colin.

Christina ran her hand along the top of the chair. Its chocolate brown cloth cover was worn a bit thin. She and her brothers had made good use of it as they grew up, fighting to see who would take their nap in it on Sunday afternoons, using it for a springboard to jump onto the sofa, hiding behind it when their mama looked for them with judgment in her eyes and a switch in her hand. Only on Christmas Eve, the one time each year when they all got together, did they leave it unoccupied.

Christina made sure of that. From the very first Christmas after her daddy's death, she had enforced that rule with an iron fist. Since their daddy had just died, it didn't seem right for anyone to sit in it that first Christmas. Though she didn't know much about such things, it seemed to her that her daddy might need that recliner, that his spirit might want to join the family by the fire, that he might snuggle down in it and share the warmth of the holy day with them.

Given her superior age and overwhelming size, her brothers let it go—even after both of them outgrew her by almost a foot and even after they all married and left home. Everyone implicitly understood the rule. At Christmas, they left the recliner for Daddy. They met on Christmas Eve, exchanged gifts, ate dessert, talked awhile, and then dispersed back to their own homes to do their own individual family celebrations. And Daddy's chair stayed empty.

Boo nudged Christina's shin again and whined plaintively, reminding her of where she was—home for Christmas, home sixteen miles outside of Brevard, North Carolina, home on twenty-nine acres of wooded mountainside. Brittle snow was falling outside and she, Christina Laws Johnson, was standing by a worn-out recliner aching to snuggle down in her daddy's lap just one more time.

Christina patted the chair, trying to make herself move, to find some matches and start the fire. But she couldn't, at least not yet. Her memories were still too strong, too heavy. As if constrained by shackles too thick to break, her thoughts kept running, running backward to days gone by. . . .

She had squeezed into her daddy's lap more times than she could even recall, his thick arms hugging her so hard she thought she would explode. As he hugged her, he also stroked her hair, his callused hands somehow smooth and gentle against her scalp. Best of all, he sang to her as she snuggled down beside him in the chair, whispering made-up lyrics quietly into her ear.

Christina felt a lump in her throat as she recalled the songs. Of all the things she loved about her daddy, she missed the songs the most.

He made up the words and they were silly, pulled from what seemed like a bottomless well of childish playfulness. The words he sang for Christina were specifically chosen just for her. Yes, he made up other songs for Colin and Cory but those were their songs and hers were hers. She liked that—her words belonged to her and somehow, though she never said it out loud, she just knew that her daddy saved his best lyrics for her tunes.

Christina smiled slightly. Truth was, Jubal Laws couldn't sing a lick. But that didn't matter to her. In her ears, his voice sounded like it came from angels. One of those songs she never forgot. Whenever she got a bit lonely or discouraged, it came back to her, a lilting encouragement ringing through her soul. He sang it to the tune of "Sweet Little Jesus Boy," the African-American spiritual so often sung at Christmas.

Sweet little Christina girl,
She is my precious baby.
Sweet little holy child, she is my precious girl.
I love to hold her close to me.
I love to see her smile.
I love to hold her close to me and squeeze her for awhile.
Sweet little Christina girl,
She is my precious baby.
Sweet little Christina girl,
She is my precious child.

Her Daddy wasn't exactly Rodgers and Hammerstein. And he sang more like John Wayne than Pavarotti. But, to a little girl in braided pigtails hugging up to his chest, he sounded better than anyone alive.

Her hand rubbed the back of the recliner one more time. It had been twenty-nine years since she had heard her daddy's voice. And she still missed it.

Leaving the chair, Christina squatted beside the fireplace and opened the kindling box. It was full. Beside it, a stack of dried, clean wood sat at the ready. Next to the wood, she spotted a rack of old newspapers. On top of the newspapers, she found a box of matches.

If she hadn't been so thoroughly depressed, she would have smiled. Just as the recliner reminded her of daddy, so this well-supplied kindling box and fireplace reminded her of her mama and her "more recent grief." The ordered precision of the wood, newspaper, and matches said as much about her mama as anything anyone could ever say.

She pulled a stack of kindling out of the box and laid it on the grate in the fireplace. Stuffing a handful of the newspaper under the kindling, she struck a match and stuck it into the paper. Within seconds, the paper caught and the fire blazed up. She threw a couple of good-sized logs over the kindling and watched for a few minutes as the logs began to burn.

Inwardly, Christina nodded. Trained as a nurse in the U.S. Army before she met Jubal Laws, her mama lived like the soldier she had been—neat and prepared, never caught by surprise. Prim and proper, buttoned down. Hair never mussed, lipstick always fresh, blouse without wrinkle, and fifteen minutes early to every appointment she ever made. Though she had never been a Girl Scout, Christina's mama Catherine did by nature what the scouts taught as lessons to be learned.

On one level, Christina had always admired that quality in her mama. Her military demeanor guaranteed that the house ran smoothly. Her daddy liked that and so did the children. It allowed her daddy to have both the time and the emotional space to act the kid, to play, to sing and laugh. Not that he didn't work hard just like her mama, and not that she didn't play and sing and laugh with him and the children. But both her parents had their own particular personality and, where one majored in one trait, the other minored, and vice versa. It worked well while both lived. They were like railroad ties and steel rails on a train track. Both were necessary and both were appreciated.

But, unfortunately, it seemed to Christina that her daddy's death had pounded out a harder edge to her mama's natural tendency toward order. Where before his passing, her mama would let down her hair and lean on her husband's shoulder and sit by the fire and sing and laugh with everyone else, after it, she pinned back her hair and sat rigid in her rocker and hardly ever broke a smile. She became even more precise, more tightly controlled. It was almost like she decided she couldn't afford any softness anymore, that relaxation or frivolity was some kind of luxury that only the most fortunate could enjoy.

Christina thought she understood her mama's predicament. With three kids, nine cows, more chickens than she could count, a full garden, little money, and no husband, her mama had to stay organized to survive. Without organization everything would have fallen apart. To Christina's sadness though, the same precision that her mama brought to her chores as a household manager also bled over into her mothering. And that was tragic. It made her mama seem remote and cold, efficient but not warm, steady but not approachable, not even by her oldest child.

Christina knew that her daddy's death had caused so much confusion in her own mind and heart that she carried an unfair bias about her mama. But, even as tragic as it sounded, she could recall her mama spanking her far more times than she could remember her mama patting her on the back.

It wasn't that her mama spanked her often. She didn't. But neither did she caress her often. Instead, she stayed apart, an ice queen as chilly as the snow falling outside.

Christina snapped her fingers at Boo and the little collie jumped into her arms as she bent over to pick him up. "I'm just like her, Boo," she said, admitting what she had known for years. "I'm just like Mama."

Boo licked her fingers as if saying that was okay by him. But it wasn't okay with Christina. She had always looked like her mama, a head taller than a broom and eight to ten pounds heavier than two sacks of fifty-pound coal. Eyes and hair the color of pine straw, a chin with just a bit too much point to it for her taste and skin that tanned a nut brown in the summers. Never a beauty pageant winner, but pretty enough to claim her fair share of attention from the mountain boys who went to school with her.

As much as she looked like her, though, Christina knew she acted like her mama even more. Quiet in crowds, not given to unnecessary conversation or big body movements, tightly wound in the emotions department. Though she often wished she could act more like her daddy, she usually ended up responding just like she had always seen her mama do.

Sighing, Christina dropped Boo to the floor and stretched, then went to the thermostat and nudged up the control switch. Boo followed her like a child afraid of getting left at the airport, a familiar trait of his. With the dog trailing behind, Christina stepped to her daddy's recliner, lifted the afghan that lay on it, sat down, and snuggled the afghan over her shoulders. Boo lay down beside her feet. She checked her watch. If she knew her brothers well, and she did, she knew they wouldn't arrive for about an hour. Like her mama, Christina tended to get places earlier than necessary. And, like her mama after her daddy died, she was, this Christmas at least, very much alone.

Staring into the fire, its heated flames dancing in her dark brown eyes, she felt herself doing what she had fought desperately to avoid in the two weeks since her mama's death. She found herself remembering the last time she saw her . . . the last time she talked to Catherine Cornelia Laws.

Chapter *2*

BAD NEWS

hristina had seen her mama alive for the last time exactly eighteen days ago. Leaving Boo with a neighbor, she had driven the thirty minutes from her house to her mama's on a brightly lit, but chilly Sunday afternoon. Since she visited her almost every Sunday, Christina hadn't bothered to call ahead.

As usual, she found her mama in the den by the fireplace, dozing in her rocker, her gray-streaked hair pinned up behind her ears, a dark green afghan thrown over her knees. Her wire-rimmed glasses lay squarely in her lap on top of the afghan. Christina smiled when she saw her. Though sitting in a straight-backed wooden rocker, her mama still dozed neatly, not a gaping mouth, not a misplaced strand of hair, not a choking snore in sight or sound.

Christina touched her on the shoulder and her mama instantly awoke. "You want a cup of tea?" she asked, not missing a beat.

"Sure," Christina said, not deviating from the weekly patter. "I'll get it."

Her mama nodded, folded the afghan, placed it neatly in the rocker, and walked to the dining room. By the time Christina had heated the tea in the microwave, thrown another log on the fire, and carried the tea to the table, her mama had pulled out two chairs, opened the curtains in the dining area, and taken a seat. It was just the two of them. Though Colin and Cory lived only about an hour away, they didn't get home nearly as much as Christina did.

Not that she blamed them too much. As the oldest child and the only daughter, it seemed natural for most of the care for her mama to fall to her. Even if they didn't communicate that well anymore.

Sitting at the kitchen table, the blue-checkered table-cloth under the heavy mugs that held their tea, Christina sighed heavily. What she had to say this week would make her relationship with her mama even worse, would upset the comfortable routine into which they had fallen over the years even more. It would ruin the dinner her mama always fixed for her, typically the spaghetti she loved so much. But she couldn't help it. The time had come to reveal the bad news.

Heavy sunlight streamed in from just beyond the wispy drapes that hung over the windows. But Christina felt dark. After sixteen years of marriage, she had decided to leave her husband Bud. True, she had left him twice before, once for eleven days and again, three years ago, for two months. This time, though, she felt certain she wouldn't go back. In her mind, she had tried everything—self-help books on relationships, video seminars with marriage gurus, in-depth counseling with two different therapists, and more late-night conversations than any married couple ought to have to endure. But nothing worked and now she had come to the conclusion that nothing ever would. She saw no other option except to make things final and get a divorce.

It wasn't that she thought Bud was a bad man, as most people define that term. He wasn't. He didn't drink much, never smoked, never committed adultery (as far as she knew), and never abused her in any way—physically or otherwise. Sometimes, perversely, she almost wished he had. At least then she would have felt something, even pain. And, maybe even more importantly, she would have known that Bud felt something too. That was the most difficult part for her—she couldn't tell if he felt anything either. When they argued, they sounded as calm as two accountants discussing a differing tally on an audit sheet. Passion was definitely not Bud's strong suit.

He worked his ten-hour days in a Brevard law office, drove home in his navy, always-clean Grand Marquis, puttered around in the woodshop he kept in the garage, and fell into bed. Every two weeks, as regular as the Saturday morning washing of the Marquis, he approached her on a Friday night for a night of calm romance. Steady but a bit too robotic for Christina.

She knew, of course, that many women would have

accepted Bud without qualm. After all, what wasn't there to like? He was reasonably handsome at six feet even and 183 pounds; reasonably successful at about $85,000 per year, and reasonably attentive to her needs. He never forgot a birthday or anniversary. He had the word "reasonable" stamped across his square forehead as surely as a hound dog has fleas on its back. So, Christina knew she should have been reasonably happy. But she wasn't.

Almost from the beginning, she felt in her bones that she had made a mistake in marrying him. But he fit her, or so she thought at the time. Having spent so much of her life feeling responsible for her two brothers, she wanted someone to take care of her for a change. And Bud certainly fulfilled that need. He took care of everything except what she had since discovered she needed most. Bud didn't know how to play.

From all that Christina could see, no art resided in Bud's soul, no imagination burned in his bones, no made-up songs fell from his lips. He lived a sterile life, as clean and unwrinkled as the starched white shirts he wore to work every day. He was simply too comfortable for her, too reasonable in almost every respect.

Strangely enough though, when she looked at Bud, she also saw much of herself. And that, though she didn't realize it at first, made their marriage empty from the start. With both of them flying on auto-pilot, the trip became pretty dull pretty fast.

For a while, Christina thought she could accept the marriage for what it was—a desert of a relationship, a union without heat. But four miscarriages, turning forty, and a layoff at the newspaper where she had begun a journalism career at the age of thirty-seven, had jolted her into a few realizations. Almost overnight, she came to the understanding that she had started to dance with middle age, and death stood next in line to cut in. If she wanted anything more than a slow waltz with "reason-ableness" she had better begin to play some new music. And soon!

So, sitting at the table, sipping her tea, Christina tried to explain all this to her mama. She knew, even as she spoke them, that her words sounded trite, even harsh. She sounded like any one of millions of women, and men too for that matter, who, staring at sagging waistlines and spreading crow's feet, decide to go out and "find them-selves." She didn't really expect her mama to understand it all. But her four miscarriages had left her feeling as dead as the babies she had named but had not delivered, the babies she had loved but never touched, the babies whose voices she had never heard, whose laughter she had never shared, whose . . . well, she felt dead, no other way to say it. And Bud's measured response to it all, his total lack of emotive capacity, piled the dirt on top of her stone-cold soul. Her only hope for resurrection lay out-side the marriage, outside the ordered existence that had sheltered and smothered her at the same time.

She told her mama everything, all of it. Not that all of it was a surprise. Her mama knew that she and Bud had not been happy. She knew about the second of the two separations. But she didn't know the marriage had deteriorated to this extent.

Her mama sipped her tea as Christina talked, but she didn't say anything. Her hands, wrinkled with the wear of the years, moved continuously. They fingered her mug, rubbed the front of the white apron she wore over her caramel-colored dress, pushed her wispy gray hair behind her ears, pressed her wire-rimmed glasses back up on her nose. That day, for some reason, the mannerisms annoyed Christina almost to the point of distraction. She had seen them all before, of course. Her mama was always rubbing her apron, pressing her glasses, pushing her hair behind her ears, working to keep everything in place.

And that's what irritated Christina most. She wanted her mama to react differently this time, to do something more than the ordinary, to rant and rave, to judge her, to make her feel even guiltier than she already did. She wanted her mama to give her permission to respond the same way, to yell and scream and pour out the utter agony that ripped and tore inside her soul. If her mama had unleashed her emotions, then she could have given hers some rein too. But Catherine Laws didn't. And, at that moment, Christina felt like she hated her for it.

Finished with her tea, Christina carefully sat her cup on the table and leaned back. Her story had come to an end. She felt drained, worn out, as spent as a salmon reaching a spawning ground. She waited for her mama's reaction.

Catherine captured a sprig of hair and rolled it behind

her ear. "You'll be alone," she said, her dark eyes peering over her spectacles at Christina. "You don't know how bad that is."

"I'm alone now," Christina said. "I've been alone for years."

"It's not as bad as it will be," her mama insisted.

"I know you don't approve," Christina said, softly, measuring her tone, not wanting to get into an argument with the one person whose support she wanted more than any other in the world.

"No, I'm sure I don't," her mama said. "A divorce is messy business." She wiped her hands on her apron. "Think of what people will say."

"I guess I don't care what people will say," Christina said.

"Well, I do," said Catherine. "I've lived in this little place all my life. We all have. We've got a good name in this town. A thing like this is hard to live down."

"It's not your problem," Christina said, her blood pressure rising by the second. "I'm the one getting the divorce, not you and not the boys."

"You know better than that," her mama insisted, her forefinger moving her glasses back. "What happens to you happens to all of us. It's always been that way up here. Kin is kin and no way around it. I think you need to go back to Bud and make it work. There's got to be something else you can do. Go see one of those counselors everybody is always talking about."

"We've done that already. Spent hours and hours sitting in an office full of enough ferns to start a weather system, talking to a guy wearing tinted glasses so dark you couldn't see his eyes. Bud and I have given him enough money to pay his daughter's way through college."

Her mama sipped from her tea, ignoring Christina's ill-placed efforts at humor. "Then go talk to the preacher. He's cheaper. Get back in church; you know I've tried to tell you that. I don't mean to judge, but you and Bud have been having these problems ever since you dropped out. I know—"

Christina held up her hand and cut her off. "Don't start on that, Mama. After the third miscarriage, I more or less decided to drop church out of the equation, if you get my drift."

"God was just testing you," Catherine said.

"Well, I flunked the test."

"And now you're making it worse, digging the hole deeper."

Christina bit her lip, forcing herself to stay seated. She didn't want to get into religion with her mama. She knew she would lose that battle. Her mama's faith was just like her personality—neat, tied down, and uncomplicated. That was one of the reasons Christina had rejected it. To her way of thinking, her life had gotten more complicated than her mama's simple God could handle.

"I don't see it that way at all, Mama," said Christina. "I'm doing the only thing I know to do. I'm going down for the third time here, and I don't see any other way to keep from drowning."

"A divorce is no life jacket, Christina," her mama said, standing up and waving her hands as if to dismiss a wayward child. "And I'll not abide it. Marriage vows aren't meant to be taken but once. You and Bud can work out your problems. I know you can. I've got faith in you. More importantly, I've got faith in God." She moved around the table toward Christina and placed her hands on her shoulders. Looking down at her daughter, her glasses slipped forward on her nose. She pushed them back up. "Now go home to Bud. You need him and he needs you."

For several seconds, Christina stared up at her mama. The flames from the fireplace behind her bounced off her mama's glasses, making her eyes seem alive. She appeared so sure, so confident, a woman who had survived so much, survived it alone, without a husband for the last twenty-nine years, survived by the steely resolve of a determined soul. Right now, though, Christina needed more than steely resolve. She needed a mama's soft hands, a mama's shared tears, a mama's soft embrace. But she didn't get it, not one bit of it.

A pair of tears forced their way into Christina's eyes. And then, against her will, she lost her cool. "But Mama," she cried, pushing away Catherine's hands. "My babies are dead! My marriage is dead! And I feel dead too! If nothing changes, I'll stay dead for the rest of my life! I don't want that, Mama! I want more than that. I need more than that. We all do, Mama. Don't we? Don't we all need more than that? Deserve it?"

Hopefully, she paused and waited for her answer. Tears rolled past her mouth and onto her chin. She tasted salt on her tongue. Her mama hovered over her, her eyes intense, her glasses perched primly on her nose.

"You're going through a phase," she said, slapping her hands onto her hips. "Believe me, I know, I've seen it a thousand times. Just go home to Bud. A boring man is better than no man at all."

Christina exploded out of her chair, her hands now on Catherine's shoulders. "Oh, I'm going!" she shouted, her anger overwhelming her desire to stay respectful. "I'm going, but not home to Bud. I'm getting out of here, away from Brevard, away from this house where no one feels anything; no one laughs or cries; no one hugs. I'm . . . I'm . . ."

Sputtering in frustration, Christina stepped back from her mama and clutched at her throat, her fingers landing on the locket resting against the second button on her blouse. "I need you to be with me in this, Mama," she shouted, squeezing the locket. "I need you to . . . I don't know, not to understand everything, I know that's too much to ask, but I need you to accept what I'm telling you . . . to love me through it, to tell me that no matter what happens, no matter what I do, I'm still your daughter, I'm still your baby girl and you'll support me in what I decide . . . you'll . . . you'll . . ."

Exhausted from her outburst, Christina almost choked on her words and she stopped shouting, the locket tight in her fingers.

"I know what you want," her mama said, as precise as a surgeon wielding a scalpel. "But I just can't give it to you. I can't support you in this. I want to . . . but . . . but I . . . I just can't, that's all. It's against everything I believe." With that, she twisted away from Christina, walked to the fireplace, and gazed into it, her back facing her daughter.

Christina felt like a blast of frigid air had just smacked into her. The person who meant more to her than anyone else had just turned away. For a moment, she couldn't do anything at all, couldn't talk or move. Her lungs went into vapor lock and she couldn't get a breath. The hurt she felt went beyond physical pain and became a throb that transcended anything her body had ever experienced. She felt rejected, cut off by the cold rigidity of a woman she loved more than life itself.

Suddenly, her lungs caught hold again and she gagged in a deep draught of air. In an instant, anger raked over her and her chest constricted and she almost snarled. In that moment she wanted her mama to hurt as much as she did—to feel the same ache that now ripped through her body. She wanted to slice her mama's heart as deeply as her mama had just cut through hers.

Christina clutched the locket in her fingers—the golden locket her mother had given her on her sixteenth birthday. The golden locket just a bit bigger than a quarter and shaped like a heart, the golden locket her mother had worn before her and her grandmother before her mother. The golden locket with her grandmother's initials, the same as hers and her mother's "CC" inscribed on the back of it.

With a vicious yank, Christina broke the chain that held the locket around her neck. The chain dangled toward the floor, spilling out like a stream of golden water, the locket itself balled in Christina's right hand. Then, as deliberately as she knew how, she took three steps closer to the fireplace, reared back, and threw the locket at Catherine.

The locket hit her mama between the shoulder blades and dropped to the hardwood floor by the stone hearth of the fireplace. For a second, her mama paused as if confused. But then she turned around and squatted down. Her glasses sliding forward on her nose, she picked up the locket.

"I'll keep this for you," Catherine said calmly, holding the locket in one hand and pushing her glasses up with the other. "One of these days, you'll want it back."

Without another word, she stood and faced the fire again. Blinded by rage, Christina stormed out of the house. Four days later, on a Thursday evening, her mama died. A heart attack dropped her in her tracks right beside the fireplace where she had stood the last time Christina had seen her. She cracked her glasses as she fell and they dropped off her nose, a shattered and untidy reminder of the woman who had kept everything so neatly all her life.

Chapter 3

FACING THE TRUTH

*C*hristina's family held her mama's funeral on the Saturday after her death. Bowing to Catherine's expressed wishes (Colin found a note outlining what she wanted at her funeral in her Bible) they allowed a showing of the body for only three hours that same morning. Practically the whole town came by the church to pay their respects. Everyone remarked on how good "Mama Catherine" looked, all decked out in her navy wool dress with the white lace at the throat, her glasses (an old pair Colin fished out of her dresser) perched smartly on her nose, her smooth hands folded in her lap.

Christina had to agree with their assessment of her mama's looks. Catherine Cornelia Laws did look regal— as well-preserved in death as she had been in life.

Nellie Patterson, one of her mama's closest friends tried to make a joke of her prim appearance. "Death is too messy for Catherine," she chortled. "I expect she'll look just as good on Judgment Day as she does right now." Everyone laughed and Nellie moved on down the line.

The people passed by all morning, each of them offering a parade of testimonials to Catherine Laws' saintliness. Christina stood at the end of the line, her feet as tired as the frayed burgundy carpet in the church sanctuary, her eyes dripping a constant flow of uneasy tears, her words muted the few times she spoke. As much as possible, she stayed silent. With Colin on one side and Cory on the other, she let them carry the conversations. And they did the task well—Colin taking the responsible role as the eldest son and Cory quite openly sharing his feelings, carrying on with the visitors with both loud laughter and ready tears. They had always been that way, Colin more reserved, Cory more outgoing, Colin like his mama, Cory like his daddy.

Busy with the sound of the boys' voices, no one seemed to notice Christina's silence. Thankfully too, they didn't seem to notice Bud's absence from her side. Though he was in attendance and checked in with her enough to keep up appearances, he had agreed with Christina that he would stay out of the way as much as possible. No reason to put any more strain on her than she already had. Grateful for his understanding, Christina stayed focused on the people who had come to pay their last respects to her mama.

Everyone had a story about Catherine Laws. How they admired her strength, raising three kids all by herself and all. How she went out of her way to help everyone else—the chicken casseroles she baked and delivered when young mothers gave birth; the afghans she knitted then sold at church fund-raisers; the nights she sat up with sick friends, caring for them with the nursing skills she so enjoyed using.

Hearing the stories, Christina just nodded and dabbed her eyes. Yes, her mama poured herself into her community. Yes, her mama lived a saintly life. Yes, when you look under the word "lady" in the dictionary, you'll see a picture of Catherine Cornelia Laws.

After the viewing of the body, the funeral home attendants closed the coffin, the heavy lid slamming down over her mama's face like a trunk closing on a stack of attic rubbish. Too numb to react, Christina took her place beside Bud and between her brothers on the front pew of the church, a white clapboard building about the size of half a gymnasium and unremarkable except for the big brown cross that hung on the wall directly over the pulpit.

When the service began, the preacher, the good Reverend Tyler Babcock, said exactly what everyone expected him to say. "Catherine Laws lived by the golden rule," he expounded. "We would all do well to live by the example she set for us. She is now in heaven with Jesus and with her beloved husband Jubal. If we'll only believe in Jesus, then one day, we'll go to heaven too."

The choir, fourteen of the most wretched-sounding voices anywhere on this green earth, belted out "How

Great Thou Art" and "Amazing Grace." Just like her mama had directed in the instructions found in her Bible. One thing about Catherine Laws—she kept everything pretty much within the bounds of tradition. The choir made up with enthusiasm what they lacked in harmony.

Nothing out of the ordinary happened at the funeral, but Christina wouldn't have noticed if it had. Wracked by guilt, her body felt separated from her head, and it seemed to her as if someone else sat in her seat and listened with her ears. The whole event rang hollow to her, like an empty oil drum thumped with a baseball bat.

Near the end of the service, she started to perspire. Glancing around, she noticed that everyone else seemed to be feeling the increasing heat as well. A number of people fanned themselves with the tiny bulletins the funeral director had given out as they entered. For a moment, she thought someone had turned up the furnace, but then she realized it had warmed up outside, like it does sometimes in winter in the South. She wiped her forehead with a tissue and licked her lips, willing herself to live through the next few minutes.

Fortunately, the service didn't last much longer. Preacher Babcock finished his eulogy, read another passage of Scripture, and told the congregation to bow for prayer. Just like that, the whole thing ended. Now there was nothing but the graveside service left to finish.

Standing, Christina stepped past Bud, took Colin and Cory by the elbows, marched out into the sunshine, and climbed into the black limousine furnished by the funeral home. No one spoke during the twenty-minute drive from the church back to their house where they would bury the body. As if dead themselves, neither she nor Colin nor Cory nor Bud seemed to have anything left to say.

Turning into the gravel driveway that led to the Laws' house, the funeral procession inched its way past Christina's childhood home. At the end of the drive, the cars stopped and the crowd piled out. Colin and Cory helped Christina out of the limousine. Unsteady on her feet, she held her brothers by the hand, one on each side, as they plodded up the incline that led to the top of the ridge behind the house. With Bud leading the way (just as Catherine Cornelia Laws had instructed), eight sturdy pallbearers in blue suits and red carnations hauled the casket up the hill behind them. The rest of the crowd fell into place to the rear of the pallbearers.

Christina's palms sweated into her brother's hands as she walked. The temperature seemed hotter and hotter, at least seventy degrees. She fought to keep her breathing even. By the time she reached the top of the hill, though, she had lost the battle.

Breathing heavily, she swept her eyes back down the ridge. Behind her and her brothers, the rest of the crowd puffed their way up the incline. Almost all of them had shucked their coats. A chorus of birds chirped above her head in the leafless oak to her left and the sun beat down as if determined to melt her right where she stood. She thought for a second she might faint.

Colin and Cory took her by the hands again and led her to the foot of the gravestone that sat just to the right of the oak. Gripping her brothers' hands, Christina inhaled and stared down at the grave. The headstone read, "Jubal Basden Laws." Underneath his name, she read the words, "Man of Faith."

Her eyes watering, she nodded then moved past her daddy's grave to the spot right beside it, the spot chosen years ago for her mama's final resting place. Christina and her brothers stopped dead-still. A funeral tent the color of Kentucky bluegrass shaded the hole dug into the ground for her mama. Everyone in the crowd stood up a little straighter as they gathered around the hole. Bud stepped up behind her. The Reverend Babcock called everyone to attention. Then he prayed, his clear voice cutting through the still air of the warm December day.

"O God," he intoned. "We who gather here today loved this dear woman, Catherine Cornelia Laws, and we shall miss her deeply. We shall miss her because of our love for her and because of her love for us. We shall miss her because her life made a difference in ours and ours made a difference in hers. She . . ."

The reverend kept praying but Christina no longer heard him. In an instant, she felt chilled to the bone, chilled in spite of the baking sun above her head and the black jacket on her back, chilled like someone had just immersed her in Tanahoe Creek in the worst weather of January. A cold realization suddenly washed over her, a realization she had vaguely intuited since she learned of her mama's death, but one that she had not until that second truly identified.

Yes, she had made a difference in her mama's life. She had caused her mama an incredible grief—a grief so deep that it killed her, dropped her like a stone by the fireplace she loved so much. Christina felt cold all right, as cold as an executioner standing by his handiwork at a gallows. She had killed her mama.

She shivered as Preacher Babcock ended his prayer, shivered and took her hands from her brothers' as the Reverend dismissed the crowd, shivered and shivered and shivered because she knew beyond any doubt that Catherine Cornelia Laws would still be alive if she hadn't gone home last Sunday to tell her about her plans to divorce Bud.

Dazed by the sheer tragedy of it all, Christina staggered through the hugging that followed the end of the graveside service and managed to get back down the ridge and into the house. Unfortunately, though, the day didn't end with the "Amen" at the graveside.

Instead, as Christina well knew as a daughter of the South, she and her family faced one more trial in the funeral ritual—the post-funeral dinner. As the eldest child, Christina dutifully took her spot at the head of the table. All around her, the friends and family of her mama pulled out their seats. Instead of returning to their own homes, they congregated here, at the home of the dearly departed to see how much chicken, potato salad, apple pie, and sweet tea they could consume in one long sitting. Watching them carry out the ritual, Christina almost grinned. The only things more plentiful than food at the home of a dead Southerner are company, conversation, and noisy children.

Though she was in no mood for any of this, she knew she had to see it through to the end. True, she could have said "no," could have claimed grief as her excuse and taken to bed, leaving the hosting to her two "stronger" brothers. But that wasn't in her. She had too much of her mama in her bones to do that. No strong, self-respecting Southern woman would take that way out, especially if that Southern woman had recently split up with her husband.

Sitting at the table, Christina looked over the crowd and wondered how many of them knew the full story about her and Bud. Probably most. After all, Bud had rented a small apartment and moved out on Tuesday. And, as the two of them had agreed beforehand, he had left right after the graveside service, a light peck on her cheek his final good-bye as he quietly slipped out of the crowd. People would notice that, even if they didn't know anything else. News like their breakup, even if only recently shared, didn't take long to spread in a town as small as Brevard.

She took a deep breath, courageously raised her chin, and fought off the desire to disappear, to flee to her own house. With the situation with Bud no doubt obvious to all, the people now gathered at her mama's house would see more than grief in her disappearance if she ran. They would see shame. And, though a Southern woman can, indeed is expected, to admit the first, Christina knew it was social suicide to admit the second.

So she stayed. Stayed and smiled as the neighbors trooped by and paid homage to her mother with handshakes and kisses on the cheeks and hugs around the neck. Stayed as her brothers and their families ate through three waves of food, the stack of ham and chicken and biscuits and cornbread and green beans and creamed corn seemingly becoming taller even as they worked to pare it down. Stayed until the shaft of sunlight that had illuminated the blue-checkered tablecloth in the dining room all afternoon shrunk up and disappeared.

Gradually, everyone but Colin and Christina drifted out of the room, the children to romp in the playroom on the second floor, Cory to watch a football game in the den, and Beth and Sue Ann to a spot in the living room with the neighbors who continued to dawdle. But Colin and she remained at the table, talking quietly. One of the ladies doing duty in the kitchen stepped in and flipped on a light. Colin yawned and stretched, then pulled a watch from his pants' pocket and flipped it open to check the time.

The watch glinted in the light from the chandelier. Immediately, Christina recognized the timepiece—a seventy-seven-year-old pocket watch that had belonged to his daddy and his daddy before him. Mama had given it to Colin on his sixteenth birthday, even as she had given Christina her locket. Cory also had a special gift given to him on his sixteenth birthday—a shotgun owned by her grandfather and father—their initials etched in the stock of the weapon. As she loved the locket as her most prized possession, so Colin loved his watch and Cory his shotgun.

Without warning, Christina lost her composure—as simple as that. The watch clobbered her, blindsided her with the reality of her mama's death, the reality she had worked so hard to avoid the last three days. She threw her head onto the table and pulled at her hair, wailing her lament. "Mama's dead! And I killed her!"

She heard Colin jump from his chair, then felt his arms wrap around her shoulders. She heaved as she cried, the weeping shaking her to her bones. Her mama was dead and buried under six feet of North Carolina mountain dirt and she had killed her as surely as if she had buried her alive. Still moaning, Christina stood up from the table and pushed away Colin's hands.

"My locket!" she shrieked. "Mama had my locket!"

Colin stepped back, obviously not sure how to react, not knowing what she meant. "Mama had your locket?" he asked dumbly.

"Yeah, Mama had it. You wouldn't understand. We had a huge blowup, as bad as you can imagine. I . . . I left my locket with her, threw it at her if you've got to know . . . got mad and stormed out. It happened last Sunday . . . when I told her I was divorcing Bud. She told me to go back to him, told me I was going through a phase . . . that she couldn't . . . couldn't support me because she didn't believe in divorce. I wanted to . . . to hurt her, make her feel as bad as I did. So, I . . . I went berserk, ripped my locket off my neck, I didn't want it anymore. I threw it at her, hit her in the back with it, she had turned away from me. Then I ran, got out of there, swore I would never come back . . . never talk to her again. That's the last time . . . the last time I saw her alive. She called me the day she died . . . but when I picked up the phone and heard her voice I couldn't . . . well I didn't speak, didn't talk to her. I hung up and within an hour she was dead, dead and gone and buried now up on the hill . . . up there with . . . with . . ."

Physically and emotionally spent, Christina stopped and leaned forward, her hands on the table, waiting for the judgment she felt sure would follow. But Colin stayed quiet. Long seconds passed between them. Christina gradually stopped crying and her body settled into stillness. The silence that fell on the room sounded heavier than the one at the church just before the service that afternoon. Christina looked around her, noticing for the first time really that everyone else had left.

She turned back to Colin. Still not speaking, he watched her carefully, like she imagined a psychiatrist might look at a crazed client. She felt confused by his utter quiet. Was he shocked? Furious? Unwilling to believe her?

Christina shrugged, not sure of what else to say, interpreting Colin's silence as condemnation. As far as she could tell, she had now irreparably cut herself off from her family. *They can't accept me now*, she thought, *now that they know I caused Mama's heart attack.*

Biting her lip, Christina wrapped her arms around her shoulders. In the last week, she had ended her marriage, killed her mama, and destroyed her relationship with her brothers. A convicted murderer could sink no lower.

Convinced of Colin's utter contempt and sure he would communicate that contempt to Cory and the rest of the family, she pushed up from the table and pivoted away to leave the room. As she opened the door, Colin's voice stopped her in her tracks.

"Wonder what Mama did with your locket?" he asked.

Christina paused, but only for a moment. Then, leaving his question hanging in the air, she slouched out of the room.

Chapter *4*

DISCOVERIES

T hough Christina left Colin alone in the
kitchen on the afternoon of her mama's
funeral, she didn't leave his question. Instead,
as the day ended and the night began, she
found herself more and more obsessed by it. Like
a piece of lint on a black dress, the question clung to her
every thought. Though she tried to pluck it away, it came
back over and over again. It stayed with her as the crowd,
even Colin and Cory and their families, left the house. It
stayed with her as she cleaned up the last of the dishes
left by the mourners. It stayed with her as she took a hot
shower, ate a light dinner of soup and crackers, and spent
a few minutes reading by the fireplace. In fact, by the
time she fell into bed in her old room, Boo beside her on
an oriental rug on the floor, the question had grown so
huge that it loomed in her head like a giant obsession, a
raging issue she had to settle.

What had her mama done with her locket after their
altercation?

Sleep refused to come as she squirmed and tossed on the bed. Guilt fertilized the matter and it began to grow like a gnarled and twisted root. Where *was* her locket?

As the moon crawled through the sky, her remorse watered the root and it spread out further and further in her heart, a black tangle of interconnected limbs, one leading to another and all of them gripping at her throat as if to strangle her. Where the root grew, nothing else could live. She knew that instinctively. Guilt was a killer, and it had its tentacles hooked hard into her.

By 3 A.M., the missing locket had become symbolic to her, symbolic of all she had lost in life—her dead mama, the daddy she knew far too briefly, the husband she had left, the children she had conceived but had never given life, the faith she had tossed aside. All of these were tied up in the same bundle and it suddenly seemed to Christina that losing the locket meant she had lost everything worthwhile, everything important and vital in life.

By the time the sun finally rose and she pushed herself out of bed, a sense of desperation lay draped over her. Without the locket, she was lost. Without it, she would never find her way back to anything resembling a normal life. Without it, she would never feel close to anything or anyone ever again. Her mama had worn it for twenty-six years and then had given it to her. As long as she had worn it, she felt connected to her mama, to the one person most responsible for her survival, her personality. Now, without it, she felt stripped, naked, without a clue to her real self, her true identity. She had to find that locket! If she could, then maybe, just maybe, something of what she had lost would also return.

Christina knew that notion didn't make sense in any tangible way. But that didn't matter, not really. She wasn't worried about what was rational. As the most personal item she owned, her locket connected her to the people and things she loved most deeply. Without it, she was nothing, nobody.

Pulling on a robe and bedroom slippers, Christina washed her face and brushed her teeth. Then, her jaw set, she stepped to the center of the bedroom and wondered where to start the search. In her closet? She decided against it. A closet was too impersonal, too dark and removed for her mama to keep it there. In her childhood jewelry box? Had her mama come to her room in the days after Christina threw the locket at her and placed it in her little girl's jewelry box?

Suddenly energized, Christina rushed to the dresser and yanked out the top left drawer. The jewelry box fell out as the drawer dropped off its hinge into her hands. Earrings and necklaces spilled onto the floor and rolled in all directions. Quickly, she dropped to her knees and tried to pick up the costume jewelry before it disappeared under the dresser and bed. More frantic by the second, she left what she hadn't already grabbed and pulled herself to her feet. Her breath came in short gulps and her chest heaved up and down. Though she had never experienced a panic attack, she suspected this was how one felt. The bedroom began to spin and she threw her head into her hands and tried to think. Where was the locket? Where should she look?

Staying on her feet suddenly became a battle. She threw out her hand and grabbed the wall to steady herself. *Okay, get a grip*, she told herself. *You won't find the locket like this. Take a deep breath. Work on this thing, think through it. Where would Mama put it? The locket has to be here somewhere. She certainly didn't sell it or give it away. So, check the house, one room at a time. Stay attentive, look carefully, and you'll find it.*

Feeling a nudge on her shin, she glanced down. Boo looked up at her, his tongue hanging from his mouth.

Christina laughed nervously. "You need to go outside, boy?" Boo wagged his tail. Christina caught her breath, the simple chore of taking care of her pet bringing everything back down to earth.

Taking Boo outside, she walked him for fifteen minutes. Calmer now, she led him back inside, then made a cup of hot tea, took several sips, and considered the best approach for her search. "Start in Mama's room," she decided aloud. The hardest place emotionally to search, but the place most likely to hold the locket.

With a quiet determination, she drank the last of her tea, left the cup on the kitchen table, and walked to her mama's bedroom, Boo right at her heels. To the left of the bed sat a solid wooden dresser—nothing fancy, just six drawers, three on the left, three on the right. On the top of the dresser a jewelry box similar to Christina's rested in the center. As if looking for a deadly snake, she cautiously picked up the box and searched through it. But the locket wasn't there.

Disappointed but no less determined, she moved to the dresser drawers, sorting through the clothes her mama wore every day, the skirts and blouses, jeans and socks, sweaters and undergarments. As Christina expected, the clothes lay in neat stacks, each of them resting in designated spots, none of them mixed or wrinkled. Even in death, her mama had everything in its place.

Many of the things Christina examined were familiar. She had seen her mama wear most of these clothes over and over again. Others, though, she had never seen at all. Some because she didn't wear them often, others because they were her personal lingerie—the private clothing no one saw but her. Carefully, lovingly, Christina thumbed through the pieces that had come most closely into contact with her mama's body—her slips, her undergarments, her stockings. The smell of her mama's perfume seemed to waft up from the clothing.

A strange sense of detachment washed over Christina and she felt as if she were dreaming. None of it seemed real to her, none of it seemed to fit. Her mama's underclothes were frillier than she had expected, lacier and silkier, with a variety of bright colors—purple and red and black. In Christina's mind, she had always imagined her mama in simple white cotton—plain and unadorned.

Christina smiled slightly as she searched through the dresser. Her mama had a side she hadn't suspected—nothing sinister of course—just a bit more expensive and free-spirited than she had ever known.

"Catherine Laws liked pretty lingerie," she whispered, looking down at Boo. "Good for her. I wish I had known this back then, back before . . ."

Christina halted in mid-sentence and Boo tilted his head as if wanting her to say more. But she pushed down the sad thought and focused again on her search for the locket. But she didn't find it in the dresser. Careful to put everything back into place, she turned her attention to a highboy that sat directly across from her mama's four-poster bed. Drawer by drawer she continued the inspection of her mama's possessions. But still she found no locket.

After the highboy she searched the bedroom closet, finding a variety of sweaters and coats, dresses and skirts, blouses and scarves and shoes. The shoes were laid out like foot soldiers all in a row, still in their original boxes. The clothing too hung in specific places, the skirts in league with the skirts, the dresses with the dresses, and so on and so on. Order, precision—a place for everything and everything in its place. But the locket? Nowhere to be found.

"Where is it, Boo?" she asked, rubbing him behind the ears. "Where's my locket?"

Boo wagged his tail but there was no authority in it.

"You don't know, do you, boy?"

Boo lowered his eyes as if ashamed of his ignorance.

Christina led him out of the closet and over to the bed, a king-sized oak piece that filled the center of the room. Flipping up the dust ruffle, she dropped to her knees and scanned the floor underneath. A stack of books stared back at her, a stack of black leather Bibles to be precise.

She pulled out the top one and ran her fingers over the slightly dusty cover. "Holy Bible," read the inscription. Catherine Cornelia Laws' good book.

Sitting cross-legged on the floor, Christina flipped open the front cover. Her mama's name and the date she had gotten the Bible were printed inside. Christina recognized the inscription. She and Colin and Cory had given this to her mama on Mother's Day eight years ago. It was the Bible once removed from the one she had been using when she died, the one Colin found on her nightstand the day after her death. The family gave Catherine Cornelia Laws, woman of faith, a new Bible for Mother's Day every five years. She insisted on it. "Five years reading will just about wear one out," Catherine always said, "that is, if you're using it like you should." The edges on this one were, as expected, frayed by its five years of service.

Christina thumbed slowly through the pages, noting that a number of them had notes jotted in the margins. She read a few of the inscriptions. "March 12," said one. "Sermon Title: When It Rains, It Pours." Another said, "July 3. Marks of a Great Nation." Christina nodded knowingly. Her mama had noted the date and the title of the sermon the pastor preached every Sunday.

Not particularly interested in this habit, Christina

dropped the Bible to the floor and picked up another one. Who knew? Maybe her mama had slipped the locket inside the pages of one of these Bibles. It made a certain kind of sense. Her mama spent a lot of time reading the Bible, especially when she felt she needed guidance. It would have been just like her to go straight to her Bible the day she and Christina had their blowup. When she finished reading, she might have hidden the locket in one of her old Bibles.

Christina searched through ten Bibles. Each of them was worn at the bindings and scarred with the noted reminders of all the sermons her mama had heard over the years, each of them living testaments of her faithfulness to the God she trusted and the church she loved. But, again, Christina found no locket.

Discouraged, but not distraught, she restacked the Bibles under the bed, pulled herself off the floor, and moved to the kitchen, Boo panting as he followed. If her mama hadn't left the locket in her bedroom, the kitchen made the most logical sense. After all, she spent more time there than anywhere else. She might easily have dropped the locket in a kitchen drawer or laid it on a shelf.

With her hopes rising at the prospect, Christina began her inspection. She sorted through the cabinets first, then the food shelves. After that came the broom and mop closet, the shelves for the dishes, and the space under the sink. Next, she rustled through the silverware, the pots and pans. You name it and Christina picked it up, looked under it, through it, and into it. Again, she found order and neatness, but no locket.

Sighing, she folded her arms and wondered what to do next. Stop for lunch? It was already past noon. Or search the den, then the rest of the bedrooms? If she didn't find it there, should she go to the garage and search the car? Or maybe the barn out back? Did Mama have a safety deposit box? Christina didn't know of one, but it was possible.

She started to call the bank to find out. Then a new thought hit her. She tilted her head and wondered at the possibility. It sounded plausible. Her mama might have been wearing the necklace when she died. She might have put the locket on another chain, slipped it over her head, and worn it right to the grave!

Upset by the notion, Christina snapped her fingers and Boo jumped into her arms. "It was her right if she did," she said to him, scratching his ears. "She owned the locket before I did." She dropped Boo back to the floor, sagged down at the kitchen table, and propped her head in her hands. She wanted to give up her search, but then she knew she couldn't. Her mama had promised to give the locket back to her, had promised to keep it for her until she did. Having made that promise, surely she wouldn't have taken it to the grave with her.

"But she didn't know when she would die," Christina said to no one. She tried to think back to the funeral, to picture her mama in the casket. Did she have the locket wrapped around her neck, snug against her now-cold flesh? She could see her lying there, her gray-flecked hair neatly combed in a sophisticated bun, her navy dress high-buttoned around her neck, her lips red with just a touch of lipstick. But she couldn't remember seeing the locket. Neither, though, could she remember not seeing it.

But if Mama wore it to the grave, Christina would never get it back. That is, unless she . . . no . . . she didn't like to think of that but . . . but she could have her mama's body exhumed . . . she could make the authorities raise the casket, check her body, see if she wore the locket to her final resting place.

Christina considered calling Colin and Cory, asking them if they recalled seeing it on her. But then she knew she couldn't do that. The boys had just buried their mama. Though Cory might sympathize with her, he wouldn't buck his older brother. And Christina knew that Colin would in no way take kindly to the idea of digging up his mother to satisfy some crazy notion of hers. He would think her even more addled than he surely already suspected.

Maybe she was imagining it, but it seemed to Christina that in the few days since she and Bud had split up, her brothers had seemed unhappy with her. Knowing that the two of them liked and admired Bud, she figured they now wondered about her and questioned her stability. She was sure her fight with her mama, which Colin, no doubt, had communicated to the rest of the family, would make them even less comfortable with her reasoning abilities.

Not sure what to do next, Christina moved to the stove to warm up another cup of tea. The funeral director! She would call him. Desperate, she stepped to the phone, located the number in the book, and dialed. An answering machine rewarded her efforts.

What kind of funeral home used an answering machine? A small one, she suddenly realized, one without the money to pay a twenty-four-hour secretary, one owned by one of her mama's friends, one that Catherine Cornelia had instructed the family to use years before they actually needed it.

Her hopes dashed and her alarm rising, Christina turned from the phone and faced the refrigerator. All sense of logic now deserted her. Without thinking how silly it was, how implausible that her mama might somehow have put the locket in with the frozen foods, she jerked open the refrigerator door. A renewed sense of unreality came over her again and nothing made any sense. Forgetting about maintaining the order her mama worked so hard to create, she pushed and pulled jars and drawers and pitchers from one side of the refrigerator to the other, her hands a pair of wrecking balls knocking aside everything in their way. But again she came up empty—no locket.

She stood dazed now, the chill of the refrigerator hitting her in the face. She blew on her fingers, closed the door, threw her head back, and wondered what to do next. What if her mama *had* worn her locket to the grave?

The notion of exhuming her mama's body popped into her head again. She would find out, she decided, one way or the other, if Catherine had the locket around her neck! But then she realized she couldn't do that, couldn't disturb her mama's grave to settle her own unsettled mind. Colin and Cory would fight her tooth and nail over something like that. And, to be honest, she knew she couldn't face it either. Putting her mama underground once was hard enough, much less exhuming her and having to do it a second time.

If not that, though, then what? She stepped back from the refrigerator and tilted her head to take a deep breath. The top of the refrigerator came into focus. She saw a stack of black books lying there. She counted the books—one, two, three, four—one on top of the other.

She knew what they were—her mama's cookbooks. Catherine Cornelia Laws had gathered them over years and years of efforts to find the tastiest, most cost-effective meals available to a frugal Southern family. Her mama cooked like she did everything else—with economy and efficiency. Everything always came out of the oven at exactly the right time and tasted perfectly seasoned. Christina could not, even to that day, remember a time when her mama threw out anything because "it just didn't turn out right." And her mama had collected the recipes for all of these wonderful and perfect dishes in this stack of black books.

The cookbooks weren't store-bought either. Nothing as costly as that for Catherine Cornelia Laws. No, the cookbooks were more like scrapbooks, originally empty like a photo album, but filled up over the years with the best recipes that the cooks of western North Carolina could exchange.

Christina had seen her mama use the books from time to time over the years, but she had never used them herself. Now that she thought about it, it seemed that her mama kept the books pretty much to herself, stacked on the refrigerator and out of reach when she wasn't using them.

Momentarily forgetting her locket, Christina stood on tiptoe and dragged down the books, all four of them, and lugged them over to the kitchen table. Easing into a chair, she hunched forward and opened the top book. Inside the front cover, she recognized her mama's delicate handwriting. The letters were clean and focused—as tight as if stitched together by a tailor with a steady hand.

On the left side of the first page, Christina read a name. Jubal Basden Laws. Underneath it, she saw these two words. FAVORITE DISHES. A third line named the first dish—chicken and dumplings. Below it, the recipe was listed:

One four- to five-pound hen, cut up
One tablespoon salt
Several celery leaves or one stalk of celery, sliced
One slice lemon
Six peppercorns
Rolled dumplings, see p. 11

Combine hen, salt, and water to cover in a large pot; bring to a boil. Add remaining ingredients, except dumplings. Boil ten minutes; skim surface, reduce heat and simmer until tender (about two hours), adding water as necessary.

Drop dumplings (see page 11) into pot on top of chicken pieces. Cover, simmer about thirty minutes or until cooked through. Yield: six to eight servings.

Christina's eyes slid to the page on the right and her heart jumped. On the right side, her mama had written a note, a note about a day on which she served that meal. By the chicken and dumplings recipe, Christina read this inscription:

"I fixed this for Jubal today, on our first anniversary. It's his favorite. If the Lord took me now, I'd die happy. I love Jubal dearly and three weeks ago I found out that I'm with child for the first time. I'm a little bit scared about having a baby, but with Jubal and the Lord by my side, I'm sure every-thing will be okay. So, Lord, I'm asking for your wisdom so I can be the wife and mother you want me to be."

Her eyes devouring that page and the ones immedi-ately after it, Christina read more of the notes, many of them only one or two lines, notes that covered twelve years of marriage, notes detailing the chronology of the life of Jubal Basden Laws and his wife Catherine and their children—Christina and Colin and Cory. In this book, each note was written beside recipes that Jubal especially enjoyed—recipes for his favorite dessert—banana pudding, and his favorite casserole—squash, and his favorite vegetable—green beans. At significant family mileposts—the marriage anniversaries, the births of the children, the birthdays that came and went—the entries were a bit longer, more detailed, more intimate in tone.

Minutes passed quickly as Christina read her mama's notes but she didn't notice the time. The inscriptions immersed her, telling her things about her mama and daddy that she had never known. Not aware of much humor in her mama, she unexpectedly found herself laughing at one of the entries, a note beside "banana pudding," written the day her daddy turned forty.

"We gave Jubal a birthday party at the preacher's house yesterday. Before we went over, I gave him a new tie, a red one with blue stripes. He wore it to the party. When he bent over to blow out his candles, he tipped the tie into the flame and it caught on fire. Jubal jerked his tie away from his neck and everybody started blowing on it. Preacher Babcock, sitting closest to Jubal, had a big bite of cake in his mouth. But, seeing Jubal on fire, he forgot about the cake. He took a deep breath and blew. Cake spewed out all over Jubal's shirt and tie. But the Preacher did put out the fire. It was a birthday none of us will ever forget."

Chuckling, Christina kept reading. The shadows outside the window lengthened as she turned the pages. She bent closer to the recipe book as the light became thinner. She read words of love, of companionship, of lives shared and appreciated. She got up and turned on a lamp by the table. Almost an hour later, she reached the last inscription in the Jubal Basden Laws book, another one written beside the "chicken and dumplings" recipe. The date cut like an open wound in Christina's chest— December 28—one week after her daddy's death. With her fingers caressing the ink as if touching a priceless figurine, she read these words:

"Today I fix this recipe for the last time. My Jubal is dead. A plane crash, plain and simple as that. I want the Lord to tell me why and one day, when I reach glory land, I plan to find out. For now, though, I just have to trust the Lord and stay strong in the faith. I can do that, I know I can, if the Lord helps me. I do worry about the children though, Christina especially. This hit her hard, she was such a daddy's girl and she's old enough to know how final this is. I fear for her, for her faith, that she'll somehow blame this on God, that she'll turn inward, bitter maybe. I've got to do my best to stay strong for her, not let her see my own sadness, my own questions about it all. If she sees me weak, it'll make her afraid and I don't want my baby, my precious little Christina to ever fear anything. Make me strong, Jesus. Keep me from ever showing her my own fears, my own loneliness. Keep me from letting Christina know how uncertain I can be. Please, Lord Jesus, put away my own anxieties so my babies will never worry."

Her shoulders shaking as she cried, Christina covered her face with her hands and lay her head on the cookbook. All these years, her mama had kept her grief to herself and she had done it all for her and Colin and Cory. What Christina had seen as rigid formality, her mama had seen as necessary strength. But now her mama was dead and she could never tell her that after all these years and all her confusion she now understood.

Chapter *5*

MEMORIES

*O*ver the next three days, Christina put the search for her locket aside and read the other cookbooks her mama had left behind. For now, the locket seemed secondary, needful of pursuit, but only after she exhausted the treasure trove of the annotations among the recipes.

Each child had his or her own individual cookbook. The only member of the family without a cookbook was her mama. Apparently, what her husband and children liked, Catherine Laws liked too.

Deliberately, Christina studied her mama's observations in small pieces, reading them at the kitchen table or in her daddy's recliner by the fireplace. She read a page or two here and a page or two there, giving herself time to digest the writings, to process what they meant, to understand how they affected her.

Between her readings, she took long walks with Boo, sipped cup after cup of tea, burned big fires in the fireplace, and pondered and churned and wondered. Making herself settle down, she sat for hours and simply thought about what it all meant.

As one would expect, she concentrated more on what Mama said about her than what she said about Colin and Cory. And given Christina's confused feelings about her mama, what Catherine Laws said took on incredible significance. What did her mama really think of her? When did the relationship between them begin to break down? Had she displeased her mama all her life or just in the last few years, the years after she dropped out of church and stopped pretending she had any faith left?

The entries about her began during her mama's pregnancy. She wrote briefly during those nine months, one-line prayers mostly, the prayers beseeching God for good health for herself and her unborn child. Other notes gave thanks for the miracle of motherhood and asked God to help her and Jubal succeed as parents. More than once, Catherine wondered if the baby would be a boy or girl, big or small, and who the child would look like—her or Jubal.

During the first seven years or so of Christina's life, the notes continued in that vein, fairly short, fairly simple, scattered in among the directions about how to make lemon chess pie (Christina's favorite dessert) or corn casserole (her favorite vegetable) or spaghetti (her favorite main dish). Between the seventh and eighth years, the entries lengthened a bit, took on a more intense tone, reflecting her mama's desire that her only daughter come to Christian faith. Christina smiled as she read these entries. In the South, the process of becoming a believer was called "being saved" or "trusting the Lord Jesus as your savior," and her mama used the terms often. As she moved into the second grade, then the third, her mama began to write out longer prayers, imploring God to bring her baby girl to faith while her heart was still soft and pliable. In due course, her mama's prayers became reality.

Christina sipped from her tea and remembered the experience. She had just turned nine. Her church entered a season of "fall revival," the religious equivalent of a spiritual Super Bowl. As the choir sang the hymn, "Softly and tenderly Jesus is calling, calling for you and for me," she eased out of her pew and stepped down the aisle to the front of the sanctuary and told the preacher that she wanted to receive forgiveness of her sins. She wanted to follow the Lord.

Three weeks later, Preacher Babcock gathered the congregation on the banks of the Tanahoe Creek for the spectacle of her baptism—a ritual of cleansing in the crisp, chilled waters of a foamy mountain stream. His right hand on the small of her back and his left hand extended toward the heavens, he shouted, "I baptize you, Christina Cornelia Laws, in the name of the Father and the Son and the Holy Ghost." Then he rocked her backward into the water, and the clear, cold stream rushed over her face and she opened her eyes and saw the blue of the sky through the lens of the mountain river and she truly did feel new, born again as her mama liked to say, a child of Jesus. . . .

Christina snapped her fingers and Boo ran to her feet. "Here, boy," she said, patting her lap. His tail jigging out and back, Boo obediently jumped up to join her.

"Let's see what Mama said that day," Christina said, scratching his ears. "Let's see how she saw all that." She found the entry beside the recipe for spaghetti—a dish seasoned with a sauce made from bell peppers, home-grown tomatoes, mountain mushrooms, and hamburger from a neighbor's stock. Her hands busy with Boo's ears, Christina read her mama's words.

"Christina was so beautiful today in her white robe, her black hair so like her daddy's. She tied it up in a ponytail with a pink ribbon. People say she looks just like me and I take that as the most wonderful compliment I could ever receive. This morning, Preacher Babcock baptized her in the river just below Tanahoe Creek. When she came up out of the water, the sun poured down from the heavens like a golden flashlight and it lit up her face and she looked like an angel. If I loved her any more, I think my soul would just pop wide open. Thank you, Lord, that she wants to follow you. Thank you that the circle of faith in my family remains unbroken. With all the humility I have, I ask you to keep it that way, to make my family circle as strong as a steel chain. In the name of Jesus, I pray. Amen."

Christina closed the cookbook and sat motionless in her chair. Her baptism, in many ways, reflected the high-light of her life with Mama. Only two years later the plane crash snuffed out her daddy's life and after that things began to change. Christina had gradually become more and more withdrawn, her unanswered questions and unmet emotional needs turning, unrecognized by anyone at the time, into the very bitterness her mama dreaded most. Though no one in her life knew how to define the issue when she was young, Christina's childish, uninformed understanding of God allowed no place for tragedy. And, because no one could define it, no one could help.

The plane crash that scattered her daddy's remains on the mountaintop had also disintegrated her faith. And, just as the authorities never recovered any significant part of her daddy, so she never recovered any significant piece of her Christian belief.

Hugging Boo, Christina realized what a disappointment she had been to her mama. When a heart attack killed Catherine Cornelia Laws twenty-nine years after the death of her dear husband and four days after the unfortunate episode with her only daughter, she had no doubt died wondering about the "circle of faith" she had so hoped to keep strong. Taking another sip of tea, Christina couldn't help but wonder about that circle as well.

* * * * *

For a solid day, Christina didn't go back to the cookbooks. Her emotional state wouldn't allow it. She was too afraid of what she would find there—the memories of the past forty-plus years she would reawaken. Not that all the memories were bad. Her first date, her first kiss at seventeen and a half (kids started late back then in strict mountain families), high school graduation, college, her engagement to Bud, her graduation from college, the marriage that followed—all these events and others like them awakened pleasant thoughts. But beside these joyous markers stood others also—detours, washed-out roads, dead ends. In her case, the road had taken a dark turn in her second year of marriage when she miscarried her first child at the end of the second month of pregnancy.

At the time the loss of the child seemed like only a momentary bump, painful yes, but not insurmountable. But then, spread over the next eleven years came three more bumps—each one getting cumulatively higher. By the time of her fourth miscarriage at the age of thirty-seven, the bumps had become a mountain, a mountain too high for her to climb, a mountain built of grief and anger and depression, a mountain under which she lay—broken and crushed and buried.

Maybe she wouldn't have left Bud if she had successfully given birth to a couple of children. Maybe she wouldn't have ditched her faith in God if she had become a mother. Who knew about such things? Certainly not Christina Laws Johnson, not then and not ever.

But one thing she did know. Her mama's journals would contain bits and pieces about all of this. Catherine

Laws was too honest to skip anything—whether good or bad. And, whether Christina liked it or not, so was she. She would have to read everything, all of it, page by page, pain by pain. If she ever wanted to come to terms with her relationship with her mama, she had to read the cookbook that contained her favorite dishes.

As the day ended and she prepared for bed, Christina wondered if her mama had written anything about the last day the two of them had been together, the day she threw away her locket. Almost certain that she had, she found sleep hard to come by. And, even when she finally did doze off at just past 1 A.M., her dreams were fitful, haunted by nightmares of what she might read tomorrow in the tiny handwriting of her now dead mother.

* * * * *

Christina slept until 9:50 the next morning. Boo woke her up, his plaintive whine a reminder of her responsibilities. Checking the clock, she quickly rolled up, surprised she had slept so far past her normal wake-up at 6:30. "Hang on, boy," she soothed Boo. "I'm coming."

Rubbing her eyes, she climbed out of bed and pulled on a robe and a pair of slippers. Her head ached and a sense of gloom hung on her like a fog in January. Opening the door for Boo, she knew immediately why she had slept so long but still felt so bad. Today she had to finish her mama's cookbooks, today she had to read what her mama thought about their last episode.

Leaving Boo outside, she stepped to the kitchen and fixed a cup of hot tea. Carrying it to the back door, she called Boo back inside, then pulled the recipe book with her name on it to the kitchen table and sat down. Her hands trembling, she drank a big swig of tea and took a deep breath.

Having decided to read the worst part first, she slowly turned to the last page of the book. If her mama had written about their final visit together, she would find it there.

"Okay, Boo," she mumbled. "Time to face the music. Let's see what she said."

Boo barked a tiny bark, then lay down at her feet. Christina stared at the page. For a second, a glare from the sun flooding through the window washed out the words. But then Christina shifted in her seat and the entry became clear and readable. As she expected, her mama had written about their last visit. The words were simple, completely in character with her mama.

"Christina came home today like she does just about every Sunday. But I didn't like what she told me when she came. She brought bad news today, says she's leaving Bud. I've been afraid this might happen, you could just see it coming. And I've tried to help, the Lord knows that. But I didn't know what to do, where to turn. Fact is, I was powerless to do anything. And that's a terrible feeling—awful.

"When Christina gave me the bad news, I didn't know what to say. Yes, I know what she wanted from me, what she

*needed. But I couldn't give it, I don't really know why. When
I should have hugged her close and been her mama, I stood
across the room and acted as her judge. I wanted to open my
arms to her, needed it maybe as much as she. But I didn't
know how. I didn't want her to think I approved of what she'd
done. But at the same time I did want her to know I loved
her. I was stuck, right between one and the other. So, I just
stood there, my back turned, trying to hide my weakness, my
sadness. I feel so sorry for her, but I don't know how to tell
her what I feel.*

*"I guess I've been so distant from other people for so long,
I've just plain forgotten how to be anything else. So now my
baby faces the hardest time of her life and she's all alone and
I'm to blame. Lord, will she ever forgive me? Will you? If you
will, then I make you this promise right here and now. The
next time I get a chance with Christina, I'll be different. I'll
give her the support and love she needs. I'll be her mama, as
simple as that. If I can only figure out how to do it."*

Her head aching, Christina quietly closed the cookbook and rested her chin in her hands. A feeling of nos-
talgia overcame her and the ache in her head spread to
her neck, then her back and shoulders. Almost immediately, though, she realized this pain wasn't physical. No,
this was worse than that. This ache came from deeper
within her body, from the furthest recesses of the marrow
in her bones. Inside those recesses a bleak emptiness
lurked, a black void that nothing but a mama could fill.
But that mama was gone, dead and vanished forever. It

was as if someone had taken a vacuum cleaner and sucked out all the heart from her, all the spirit that gave her life and hope.

Christina dropped her head to the kitchen table and began to cry. The sun, now a blaze of heat boiling through the drapes, warmed the tears that flowed down her face. And the sun-soaked tears made a puddle on the tablecloth—a tablecloth her mama had made with her own hands.

Chapter

EXCHANGING GIFTS

hristina had read the last page of her mama's cookbook diaries seven days ago. Now, it was Christmas Eve and she had come back home once more, maybe for the last time in a long time. She sat in her daddy's recliner by the fire, a tan afghan over her legs, waiting for her brothers and their families to arrive for what she expected to be a tense Christmas Eve celebration.

She had pretty much given up on finding the locket. After finishing her reading of the cookbooks, she had continued the search the next day. She rustled through everything in the house one more time, then turned her attention to the car, the garage, and the barn in the back-yard. With no luck in any of those places, she called the bank about the safety deposit box, but found out her mama didn't have one.

Finished with the intensive inspection, Christina felt fairly confident that her mama hadn't left it at the house.

If she had, she would have found it. Maybe she really did have it around her neck, Christina concluded, buried forever, the gold heart nestled near to her soul, unable to keep her promise to give it back because she died before an opportunity came.

Christina pushed up from the chair, dropped a log onto the fire, and decided to let it rest. If her mama was wearing the locket, then okay. She snapped her fingers and Boo sprung up from the floor by the recliner, his eyes alert.

"I can live with that," said Christina, scratching her pet. "Maybe that's the best thing anyway. Let the locket stay there, next to Mama's heart."

Boo wagged his tail in agreement.

"I think I understand her a little better now, now that I've read her diaries."

Boo barked softly as if he understood too.

Hearing a car pull up, Christina stood from the fireplace. By the time she reached the window to look outside, a second vehicle had joined the first one. A minute later, a series of thumps and whoops sounded through the snow and then a whole tribe of blond-headed kids poured through the door, their scarves and hats flying in all directions as they peeled off their winter gear.

Boo, completely out of character, gave up his timidity when he heard the kids approaching. Showing a complete lack of discernment, he ran into the stack of kids with a fervor Christina could in no way match. The sheltie's tail wagged furiously and his tongue licked in and out, landing on patches of exposed skin wherever he could find it.

Though reading her mama's cookbooks had taken the edge off the worst of her bitterness, Christina knew she still had a long way to go before she could greet her brothers' kids with such enthusiasm. The resentment she had built up toward her brothers' much-blessed lives wouldn't go away quite that easily. After all, the big "D" of divorce still scarred her chest, and her mama had died thinking she hated her. Not exactly a recipe for Christmas cheer.

Forcing herself to hide her feelings, Christina chiseled a smile onto her face and hugged all seven of the kids in turn. Finished with them, she worked her way through her sisters-in-law and brothers. The family did it every year in exactly the same way, the predictable nature of it all providing both a comforting ritual and a sense of dull routine. In spite of everything, Christina found herself warming to the pack as she patted each one and said her "hellos." She did love them, after all, and they were all she had.

Feeling more pleasant than she expected, she turned away and got busy with the preparations for the annual gift exchange. While Colin hauled in a stack of presents and arranged them around the tree and Cory hauled in more firewood, she joined Beth and Sue Ann in the kitchen. Working as a team, they made coffee, unwrapped cakes and pies, and set the table. Within min-utes, the place literally pulsed with the sights and sounds of the season. Bing Crosby sang "I'm Dreaming of a White Christmas," from a small CD player Cory had brought, and the logs in the fireplace cracked in time to the rhythm of his voice. The aroma of wood smoke and Christmas tree and hot cider and apple pie fought for the attention of everyone's nostrils, and the kids romped and ran with Boo.

Calling Brad, Colin's oldest boy, a seventeen-year-old six-footer, Christina sent him to her four-wheeler to bring in her contributions to the mound of packages that threatened to dwarf the tree her mama had so carefully put up and decorated in anticipation of the family gathering. They celebrated this way every year, bringing their gifts to the old home place on Christmas Eve for proper placement under the tree. The whole family then gathered around it—Mama in her rocker, the kids on the floor, the adults on the sofa or in a chair dragged in from the kitchen. Her daddy's recliner remained unoccupied.

On a rotating basis, as they became old enough, one of the kids read Luke 2 from the Bible. Mama would follow the Bible reading with a prayer. Then she would place the Star of Bethlehem on the top of the tree, her tiny frame standing several rungs up a ladder to reach the top.

After that, the delirium began. The youngest child who could read, and it seemed that a different one showed up every year to do the honors, acted as the master of ceremonies, picking up the packages one by one, reading off the name, then handing it over to the recipient. The children received all their presents first, then the adults.

Care was taken to open one gift at a time, again children first. After each person had seen his or her first gift, each received a second gift, then a third. They went through the whole stack that way every year—each recipient opening his or her gift while the others watched, oohing and ahhing, calling out "I hope it fits," or "That color goes great with your eyes."

The recipient stuck to the script too, yelling, "It's just what I needed," or "I can't wait to try it on," or "Who's this from?"

The whole thing—twelve people receiving three or four gifts apiece—usually took about two hours. To get a gift at the Laws house, you had to pay for it with a lot of valuable time.

Deep down, Christina had to admit she had always loved these Christmas Eve nights together. They made her feel warm and secure in ways that nothing else ever did. Best of all, she felt closest to her daddy in these blessed hours, usually allowing her memory to run free in them, to go back to her childhood, to the days when life seemed easy and she was happy.

But, sitting on the sofa by Colin that first Christmas after her mama died, she found herself sinking into a tired sadness. Christmas now held no blessedness for her, she thought, no feeling of intimacy with her daddy or mama.

Half-heartedly, she listened to Dana, Colin's ten-year-old, as she read the Bible. She looked at her mama's rocker. Like her daddy's recliner, it now sat empty too.

Working to pull herself out of the depression about to drown her, she tried to smile at Dana. But her face refused to cooperate and she didn't force it.

Dana finished Luke 2 and leaned back, pleased with her work. Christina stared at her daddy's chair. Her chin sank lower to her chest. Colin, taking her mama's place, pulled a ladder into position, lifted the star from its box where he had placed it when he arrived, climbed several rungs, and hung the Christmas star at the top of the tree. Christina watched him, but found no pleasure in it. Before his death, her daddy had held this honor. Then her mama. Now it fell to Colin, the oldest son. He stepped down from the tree and rubbed his hands together, a solemn but satisfied look on his face.

Then Brad yelled, "It's time to open presents!"

A floodgate of noise exploded in the room. Christina noticed that no one had said the prayer, but she didn't feel like saying anything. Cory's third child Stephanie, also ten years old like Dana, didn't give her a chance anyway. Instead, she stood up immediately and moved to the tree. She was the family Santa this year.

As Stephanie began to hand out the presents, the chatter in the room notched louder and louder. The sound of ripping paper and exclamations of joy cut through the den. The adults sipped their coffee or tea or cider. The kids squealed and shouted, tearing open their presents with unvarnished glee.

Doing her best to keep up with the sentiment, Christina chimed in with "you're welcome" and smiled gamely when anybody tore open one of her offerings and expressed their thanks. Having called Beth and Sue Ann in October to find out what everyone wanted, she knew her gifts would meet their approval.

The time hung on stubbornly as the children unwrapped their gifts, but somehow Christina managed to last through the whole process. She kept telling herself that she should feel good about nights like this; that her family loved her and supported her in spite of everything that had transpired over the last few days. But she couldn't know that for sure. In fact, she didn't really know what Colin and Cory and Beth and Sue Ann thought of her situation. Did they blame her for her mama's death? Maybe so. After all, she blamed herself, didn't she?

Watching them carefully, Christina decided everyone seemed okay, as normal as any family gathered on Christmas Eve. But who could know? Shaking her head to push the thought away, Christina just wished they would hurry up with the unwrapping, share their Christmas desserts, and clear out.

For a second, Christina had the horrifying thought that the snow might keep them here, that they would be unable to leave, that she would get no time by herself on this Christmas Eve. But then she remembered that it had snowed like this several times in the past, but neither Colin nor Cory had let it hold him back. They took the weather as part of the challenge, the magic of the season.

They loved to climb into their four-wheel-drive vehicles and plow their way through the icy white back to their homes. It made Christina thankful for all-terrain machines, in spite of the gas they sucked and the noise they made.

"Time for the grown-ups," yelled Cory, rubbing his hands together. "Stephanie, pass out the loot."

Christina pushed her hair out of her eyes and watched as Stephanie started the routine. Sue Ann, then Beth, Cory, then Colin. As the oldest, she brought up the rear. Each of the adults received presents in the reverse order of their birth. Thankfully for Christina, the process went faster with the adults—they got fewer presents. Within thirty minutes, they were nearing the end. The stack under the tree had dwindled down to almost nothing.

"Only a few presents left," shouted Brad.

"They're for the grown-ups," said Stephanie, intently checking the labels. "Here's one to Daddy." She picked up the present and handed it to Cory.

"You're out of order," yelled Dana. "You should get one for Aunt Sue first, then Uncle Cory, then my mom."

"But my daddy was closest," argued Stephanie. "And we're almost done."

"What is it?" asked Brad, ignoring Dana's complaint. "Who's it from?"

Everyone looked at Cory. A scowl crossed his brow. He held the present up so everyone could see it. The present was wrapped in silver paper and had a red bow around it.

"It's from your Grandmom," he said, his voice a whisper.

Christina rocked back in her seat as Colin stood up and moved to the tree. The children became briefly quiet, sensing the change of mood in the room, before Jeb, Cory and Sue Ann's youngest, wondered aloud in childlike frankness, "What about my present from Grandmom?"

"Sweetie, she probably didn't have time to wrap the grandkids' presents before she went to be with Jesus," his mother explained. "We'll talk about it later, okay?"

Colin bent over and picked up a second package, then a third. Each was wrapped in silver paper and had a red bow.

"They all from Mama?" asked Cory, joining Colin at the tree. "When did she—?"

"Obviously a few days before she died," Christina said, gathering her thoughts. "I saw her on Sunday. Anybody see her between then and Thursday?"

Colin and Cory shook their heads.

"I mailed her most of our presents," said Sue Ann. "No room to put them and the kids in the car."

"So did I," said Beth. "She must have added hers to the stack and put them all here, together under the tree."

"Just like Mama," said Cory. "Always prepared. Even though she's . . . well . . . she's . . ."

"The word is 'dead,'" Christina interjected, her voice tinged with a tremor of anger she didn't quite understand.

"Yeah, well, even though she's dead, she's still giving us something for Christmas," countered Cory, rolling his eyes at his sister.

For a moment no one said anything else. Her curiosity

getting to her in spite of her dejected mood, Christina pulled up from her chair and joined Cory and Colin by the tree.

"Well, let's open them," she said. "See what Mama left us."

She squatted down and picked up a present labeled for Colin.

Their hands quick to action, her brothers ripped into the silver paper, tossing it and the red bows to the floor. Her eyes searching for the gift with her name on it, she bent under the tree and pulled out a couple of more presents and handed them to Beth and Sue Ann.

"It's a new electric shaver," shouted Colin, holding up a box for all to see. "I've wanted one for over a year, ever since my old one locked up on me." He turned to Beth. "You told Mama, didn't you?"

She nodded her complicity. "Yeah, back in August."

All eyes focused on Cory. His box was bigger than Colin's. He ripped the top off it and his eyes sparkled as he saw the contents. "Golf stuff," he said. "Fifteen golf balls, a glove, and a subscription to *Golf Digest*. Mama knows there's nothing I like better."

For a second, everyone became quiet again. But then Brad broke the silence. "What did you get, Mom?" he asked.

"Aunt Sue Ann goes first," insisted Colin.

Sue Ann nodded and opened her gift. It was a jacket the color of dark chocolate and a matching pair of slacks.

"That'll go great with your eyes," said Beth. "And that

new necklace you showed me last week."

Sue Ann smiled and held the jacket up to her shoulders to test the fit.

"Your turn," yelled Brad, pointing to Beth. "Open it."

Inside her box, Beth found a navy silk blouse and a tan skirt.

"It's beautiful," said Sue Ann.

"Mama had good taste," said Cory.

"She spent too much," said Beth, rubbing her hand over the blouse.

"She probably saved all year to buy these presents for us," said Cory.

"Just like Mama," said Colin. "Wouldn't waste a dime on herself, but more than willing to splurge on someone else."

Watching her sisters-in-law admire their gifts, Christina felt her stomach knot up with anxiety. Her face felt hot and a rim of beaded perspiration covered her upper lip. Though she hadn't examined carefully, she hadn't seen a present for her anywhere under the tree. She knew that didn't make sense. No matter how angry her mama was, she surely wouldn't have deliberately left Christina out.

As casually as possible, she glanced once more around the base of the tree, her eyes examining the white sheeting that sat around the trunk, the sheeting that provided protection for the floor and a snowy look for decoration. But she saw no gift. No more silver boxes wrapped with red bows lay under the tall pine.

"Time to clean up," she said, hoping against hope that her brothers wouldn't notice that her mama had indeed left her out, praying that they would go on about their business without further ado. Grabbing a handful of wrapping paper, she squeezed it into a big ball. The sound of its crackling filled the quiet room.

"What did Mama leave you?" asked Colin, seemingly unaware that Christina hadn't picked up a box.

"I got it earlier," she said, trying desperately to cover her embarrassment.

"What do you mean?" asked Cory. "We didn't even know these were here. What did Mama leave you?"

Christina's breathing became ragged and she closed her eyes, wishing she could find a way out of the awful room, wishing she could float away like the smoke that rose through the chimney and into the night outside. Her mama had left her out. No way to deny it. After their fight, Catherine Cornelia Laws had disowned her, washed her hands of her faithless, worthless, disappointing daughter—despite what she had written in the cookbook.

"Nothing," she said as calmly as possible.

"What?" asked Colin.

"Children, leave the room," said Beth, her voice stern, demanding immediate response. "Go get something to eat."

For a second, Christina thought Brad was going to argue with his mom. But then Beth gave him a quick shake of her head and he gave up the notion. Following his lead, the other kids also shuffled out.

Everyone turned to Christina. Seeing she had no escape, she shrugged and decided to tough it out.

"Mama didn't leave me anything," she said, her lower lip quivering. "You know we had a fight the Sunday before she died. She couldn't accept the fact that I was leaving Bud. I told her she had no say in the matter. I guess she died before she got over it, before she had a chance to get me a Christmas present."

"Mama wouldn't do that," said Cory, pushing past her, headed to the tree. "She wasn't like that. No matter what happened between you two, she left you something, I just know she did."

Feeling more and more humiliated, Christina grabbed his arm and jerked him away from the spruce. "Leave it!" she growled between clenched teeth. "She left me out, as simple as that. Don't make things worse than they are by looking for something that isn't there! Maybe she planned to give me something later. I don't know, but there's nothing there now. I looked. Just give it up, okay?"

For an instant, Cory tensed, the muscles in his biceps bunching under his sweater. "Don't embarrass me any-more than I already am," Christina begged, fighting to hold back her tears. "Just let it go. Please?"

Cory paused, but only for an instant. Then he nod-ded, casting his eyes to the ground. Christina turned to Colin. He turned his palms up, accepting her wishes. Without another word, she pivoted and slumped out of the room.

* * * * *

Skipping the traditional desserts, Colin and Cory and their relentlessly picturesque families headed out less than an hour later. "Time to get home for Santa Claus," they shouted, their false bravado making Christina feel even worse.

"Can't miss that," she agreed, glad to see them leave. "If you're not there, Santa won't know where to find you."

"You can come with us," said Cory, lingering at the door, obviously reluctant to leave her by herself.

She patted him on the back. "I'll be fine," she said. "The noise of your children on Christmas morning might be more family togetherness than I can stand."

"Then I'll call you tomorrow," he said.

"Good, I'll look forward to it." Christina eased him out the door, then watched through the window as both vehicles slowly negotiated their way through the snow.

When their taillights had disappeared at the end of the drive, she stayed by the window only long enough to see that the snow had stopped. From what she could see, about seven inches now blanketed the ground. Twisting back to the den, she paused for a second, unsure what to do next. The fire had burned down in the fireplace, the embers now only a golden glow under the ashes. A green garland lay across the mantle. One stocking, looking lonely now that all the rest had gone, still hung above the fireplace. Beside the fireplace sat the Christmas tree, its all-white lights displaying a fake promise of Christmas cheer.

Gazing at the tree, Christina felt a sudden urge to end this whole night and put the disaster behind her. Okay, she concluded, her mama had left her out. Nothing she could do about it. As her daddy used to say, "Life sometimes cooks up some hard biscuits."

With Boo at her heels, she trudged across the room and pulled the stocking down. The garland hanging on the mantel followed the stocking. Grabbing a box from the hallway past the kitchen, she stuffed the garland and the stocking into the bottom.

Flushed with adrenaline now that she had a plan, she carried the box back to the tree and began pulling off the ornaments—the lights, the bells and baubles, the strings of beads and peppermint sticks. Too depressed to care much about protecting them, she dropped the decorations unceremoniously into the box. The pile grew higher and higher as she stripped away the pieces that had always before given her such great pleasure.

But she didn't want to see them anymore. Right now she wanted any and all reminders of Christmas out of her sight, back in the closet, out of her mind. This year the decorations seemed to point a finger at her; they seemed to shout that her mama had cut her off forever and she would never have the chance to make things right again.

Her hands moving faster and faster as her emotions took over, Christina ripped the rest of the decorations from the tree. The job didn't take long. Within minutes, the chore was almost done. Only one ornament left, the ten-inch high glass star stuck right on the top.

For a second, she stopped and stared at the star. Every year of her life she had seen it there—perched at the top of the tree, the last ornament on and the last one off, the symbol of her family gatherings at Christmas, the symbol of everything being in place, everything being together.

Gritting her teeth, Christina scooted over the ladder and climbed onto it. Tears pushed at her eyes, but she fought them off. Nothing was in place this year, nothing was together!

On her tiptoes, she picked the star off the tree. With a quick glance down, she descended the ladder. Tears blurred her vision. She stumbled two steps from the bottom and the star slipped from her hands. Fighting to keep her balance, she grabbed at the star but missed and it fell toward the box of tangled decorations sitting on the floor. With a loud crash, the star landed squarely in the center of the pile, its glass cracking into a thousand pieces as it hit the unyielding stack of ornaments.

The sound of the breaking glass tipped Christina over the edge and the emotion she had tried so hard to keep bottled up while her brothers were there now poured out. She felt like the star, shattered into a million pieces, her life broken by all the tragedy she had experienced, by all the grief . . . all the loss. Pulling up straight, she bit her lip to keep from crying even more and felt guilty and angry at the same time. Nothing good had ever happened to her, nothing good at all. At her feet, Boo whirled around and around in a circle, his senses obviously picking up the intensity in his mistress.

Her face red with hurt, Christina bent over and stared into the box, her mind reeling. For a second she imagined she could fix the star, pick up the pieces and glue them together, forget she had ever broken it, and use it again next Christmas and every Christmas after that. But then she saw it once more, busted and broken and . . . and forever destroyed.

At her ankles, Boo looked up at her, his face a sad mirror of her own. Gathering herself, Christina bent down and rubbed him behind the ears. The anger she had felt a few moments ago now dissipated into a melancholy fatigue.

"It's a mess, boy," Christina said. "A royal mess."

Boo whined softly. Christina stood again, her eyes clear once more. Then, her mind calmer but no less heavy, she stepped to the Christmas tree and wrapped her hand around the trunk.

"Let's get it out," she said wearily to Boo. "Get it out of the house. Then we'll leave, once and for all."

Christina yanked the tree toward her, bending it almost parallel to the floor. Taking a step back, she pulled it harder and it toppled over, water from the holder sloshing everywhere. The treetop pointed like a knife toward her face. Taking a deep breath, she jerked the spruce again and backed up three steps. The tree slid after her toward the door, the white sheeting at its base trailing across the hardwood floor like a cheap train on a bridal gown.

Get rid of the tree! she thought, tensing her muscles, anxious now to finish the job and get home. *Get rid of it and get out!* She heaved again and the tree moved another few feet.

At the door, Christina reached back and pulled it open and a slap of cold air stung her face as she stood in the gaping doorway. Facing the tree again, she realized she couldn't get it through the door the way it was facing. With the top at the door, the wider branches near the bottom would catch on the doorframe. To get it out she had to turn the tree around and take it out bottom first so the branches could fold inward rather than outward.

Impatient with the delay and snorting her disgust at her own stupidity, Christina stepped to the bottom of the spruce and took a handful of the white sheet into her hands. A couple of good jerks and she could turn it around, move the tree to the yard, leave it behind, leave it all . . .

She tugged hard on the tree bottom.

The trunk moved sideways, clockwise.

She pulled again.

A silver box fell out of the sheet in her hands. Christina saw a red bow wrapped around it.

Christina froze in her steps, the box at her feet.

Several moments slipped by. The wind whipped in from the porch and across her face, pushing her hair into her eyes. She flipped the hair away and stared down at the box, afraid to touch it, but also afraid to leave it alone.

What if it wasn't for her? What if her mama had left it for one of her many friends? The preacher maybe? Her mama gave him and his wife a gift every year.

Christina continued to stare at the box, her knees

trembling, her hands still clutching the trunk of the Christmas tree. The box was rectangular in shape and about the size of a bar of soap.

Behind her, she heard Boo whine. He nuzzled up against her legs to avoid the wind from outside. "Okay," she said to Boo. "I have to do this. I have to know; I have to find out what Mama left in that box!"

Boo barked his agreement.

Her hands shaking, Christina dropped the tree trunk and bent over to the floor. Picking up the box, she closed her eyes for a moment, then opened them again, and quickly read the card stuck to the silver wrapping paper.

"To Christina."

"From Mama."

Slamming the door, Christina dropped to the floor beside the Christmas tree and ripped off the silver wrapping. Inside the paper, she found a white box. Inside the box she found a piece of paper, all folded up. Under the paper, she saw a golden locket.

Her heart rose to her throat. She picked up the paper in one hand and the locket in the other. Quickly unfolding the paper, she recognized her mama's handwriting, neat and small. The paper unfolded into an eight by eleven piece of notebook paper, nothing fancy. But that didn't matter to Christina. Her eyes darted to the beginning of the note.

"Precious Christina. Here's your locket. I know you surely want it back and I'm glad to give it. When I thought about what to give you for Christmas, I couldn't imagine anything

better. I know now I hurt you deeply when you came to me about Bud. I'm sorry I didn't react differently and I don't know why I did what I did. I don't approve of divorce, you know that, but that wasn't the vital issue last Sunday, wasn't what was most important. And I failed you miserably.

You may not believe this, but I can remember a time when I wasn't so closed off . . . so, I don't know . . . so unable to express the love I feel deep inside me. But after my Jubal died, something in me shut down, as if someone had turned off the water in a faucet. I dried up, became afraid of showing what I really felt, afraid of getting too intimate with people, too close to them.

I think that's why I never married again. I was just too scared to love a man again and take the chance of losing him. Sadly, though, my fear of losing someone I loved caused me to lose you. When you and I had our 'scene' a couple days ago, the irony of it all suddenly hit me. By being afraid of loving and losing, I quit loving at all. I know now that I can't really do that—love without letting go, love with my arms folded and my back turned. But that's what I've tried to do all these years. And I'm just now understanding that. I guess I'm a slow learner.

When you threw your locket at me, it was like a hammer in my back, breaking through the shell I had built up around myself. It's a hard way for such a thing to happen, but you did that for me—your anger, really, your hurt. It finally busted through and I saw it all for the first time. By trying to protect myself, I have separated myself from those I love the most.

I cried all night after you left. I wept on my bed and held

your locket in my hands. For the first time since my Jubal died, I let myself feel my own aloneness. I realized as I cried that I didn't want to be alone anymore. I want to know you, to stand by you, to be what you need me to be as you face this dark time in your life.

For me to do this, though, means I have to ask you do something that I have no right to request. It means I have to ask you to forgive me. I have to ask you to give me the mercy I refused to give you.

Ironic, huh? I need what I didn't give—forgiveness.

So, that's what I want from you for Christmas this year. Forgiveness. After all, that's what the season is all about, isn't it? I can't imagine a better gift, or a more costly one.

I know I don't deserve it. So you'll have to decide. And I expect it'll take awhile for it to work out completely. Forgiveness is a process, after all. But I'm asking you to give me this gift for Christmas—the gift of a new start, a new chance to be your Mama.

I hope you'll put on your locket tonight after we all open our presents (I got the chain fixed where you broke it). If you put it on, then I'll know you want to try and I'll be grateful to you for it.

Either way—remember this. I do love you and I plan to use the rest of my life to prove it.

May the Lord Jesus wrap his arms around you, my precious Christina, and hold you close.

Love and Merry Christmas,

Mama

Finished with the note, Christina didn't move for several seconds. Instead, she sat and stared into the last of the fire, the locket tight in her fist, the Christmas tree on its side on the floor. Boo waited at her feet, his head on his paws. A clock on the mantel clicked as the big hand shifted to cover the little hand.

Hearing the click, Christina looked up at the clock. It was midnight—Christmas Day had begun. The day of birth, the day of new beginnings, the day of hope and love, the day of Jesus.

She stood up and squeezed the locket in the palm of her right hand. Boo stirred and stood too.

Christina's face flushed as she thought of her mama's request. Forgiveness—that's what her mama wanted. It sounded so simple—just wrap it all up in a silver box and top it off with a big red bow.

Christina's eyes swept across the room and landed on her mama's rocking chair. A flood of memories washed over her, memories of all the nights her mama had sat in that chair, all the Christmases the family had shared, all the chances for intimacy she and her mama had passed up. Chances to love and care for each other. She and her mama and her brothers had misspent so many of those chances, had let them slip through their fingers like so much water over a dam.

They had acted as if the supply of chances were endless. But how wrong they were, all of them, spendthrifts of the currency of life. So now they were broke, poverty-stricken, paupers with empty pockets. And not because they had spent their chances well, or invested them wisely. No, they were broke because they had thrown all the chances away, her and her mama and her brothers. They had thrown them away as if they were trash, common garbage worth nothing more than hauling to a landfill. But now her mama wanted her forgiveness for her part in the wastefulness.

Her heart pounding, Christina left the tree on the floor, walked past it and back to the front door. Her jaw firm, she threw open the door and stepped onto the porch. Ignoring the cold that blasted her face, she eased off the porch and into the crust of white that lay on the ground. Ever the coward, Boo stayed in the house and whined.

Christina sunk to her ankles in the snow and her shoes almost sucked off when she lifted her legs out. But she didn't care anymore. Her adrenaline keeping her warm, she plunged forward into the freezing night, her breath pouring out in white puffs, her arms out to the sides to give her balance.

Overhead, the snow clouds had scuttled away and the sky had cleared. Now, it twinkled, a black canopy dotted with stars as bright as Christmas lights. Getting farther and farther from the warmth of the house, she heard Boo's whining growing more distant. For a split second, she paused and twisted back to look. The house seemed so snug, its lights in stark contrast to the black evening. The door stood open, Boo framed in the wash of light.

Her tracks leaving a trail between the trees that surrounded the yard, Christina pivoted and moved through the snow to the back of the house. The ground beneath her feet shifted and became steeper as she reached the backyard. Catching her wind, she bent forward at the waist and pushed herself up the hill that led past the barn and away from the house. Her feet were numb now, frozen by the snow.

Christina worked harder as the hill became steeper still. She stumbled on a rock buried in the icy white and almost fell, throwing her arms forward into the snow to catch herself. She almost dropped the locket. At the last second, though, she squeezed her fist and clamped the treasure in her fingers.

Her arms and hands tingling from the wet snow, she pushed up and pressed ahead. Only a few more yards and she would reach her destination: the top of the ridge on the hill outside the back of the Jubal and Catherine Laws home place.

She stepped onto the ridge and fastened her eyes on the leafless twin oaks that framed the family burial spot. A layer of white lay in the nooks of the tree branches, thick blankets of frigid powder. Beyond the tops of the trees, the stars gazed down on her as if curious to see what she would do next. Her heart thumping wildly, she stepped past the oaks and pushed to the graves where her mama and daddy lay buried in the crusted, icy night.

The locket clutched in her fist, Christina stopped at the feet of her mama's tombstone. Her breath came in ragged gasps. The sweat that covered her face felt like it was beginning to freeze. She hugged her arms around her waist and tried to clear her thoughts.

Her mama had asked for forgiveness for Christmas— said if she put on the locket, she would know her only daughter had forgiven her.

Christina's blood pounded in her temples.

Before she could forgive her mama, she had to forgive herself. But she didn't know if she could do that.

Her fingers tightened even more on the locket.

To forgive herself, she had to receive the forgiveness God offered to her. But she didn't know if she could ask for that.

Tears pushed to the corners of her eyes.

Could she do that—ask God for forgiveness?

She remembered the words of Jesus from the cross. "Father, forgive them, for they know not what they do."

Christina fell to her knees on her mama's grave and lifted her head toward the stars.

The tears came steadily, their warmth in sharp contrast to the winter air.

She lifted the locket into the air.

She thought of her mama. She thought of her daddy. She thought of Bud.

She untangled the neck chain of the locket and held it in a golden arc above her head.

She thought of her loneliness and the weight of guilt that pressed down on her soul.

The tears became a torrent now, a gush of remorse and repentance rolling down her face, off her chin, and into the snow that encased the earth.

She dropped the chain and the locket around her neck. The locket fell to her chest, then nestled there softly, comfortable in its proper place.

Closing her eyes, Christina threw out her arms and fell forward, her face into the snow, her arms outstretched in a wide-spread embrace of her mama's grave, her warm tears alighting on the brittle snow and melting it where the two mingled.

And there on the ground, as she hugged her mama's final resting place, she gave Catherine Cornelia Laws the gift she wanted for Christmas. She gave her mama the gift of forgiveness, the last gift she could ever give.

As she forgave her mama, Christina also realized what her mama had given to her. By asking for her forgiveness, her mama had brought her to the feet of Jesus to ask for his upon her own life. And just as surely as Christina forgave her mama, she knew that God had also forgiven her.

Above Christina's head, the stars shone down like a billion smiles and the cold of the night dropped still further. But Christina didn't notice any of that. She didn't notice because her arms were still outstretched on her mama's grave and her heart was full and she felt warm and free.

CHRISTMAS SURPRISES

TEN YEARS LATER
CHRISTMAS EVE

itting in her mama's old rocker, Christina turned the page of the journal she held in her hand. Then, adjusting the reading glasses that perched on the end of her nose, she touched pen to paper again and continued to write.

"Ten years have passed since the Christmas night I found my locket and I turned fifty in October of this year. It's December twenty-fourth and I'm sitting at home again for Christmas. Boo is at my feet, twelve years old now, slow to walk and almost blind, but no braver than he ever was. Colin and Cory are sitting across from me, Colin in a kitchen chair and Cory in Daddy's recliner. That's right, in the recliner.

"The Christmas after I found my locket in the silver box with the red bow, I suggested a few changes in our routine.

After a bit of discussion, Colin and Cory agreed that what I said made sense. Now, my brothers sit in Daddy's recliner on a rotating basis—Colin one year, Cory the next. Looking at them now, they look so much like Daddy, I can almost imagine him sitting there, a big grin on his face, singing a made-up song, off-key as always.

"Bud is sitting beside me. That's a surprise, I'm sure. It certainly was to me. But an amazing thing happened after the Christmas Mama died. I started to change. My emotions, bottled up for so long, began to bubble up from under the surface. It just seemed I couldn't hold back my feelings anymore. They demanded that I deal with them, one way or the other. So I did, gradually at first, but then more and more completely.

"As Bud and I met to work out details of our divorce, I unexpectedly found myself attracted to his strength, warmed by the gracious way he dealt with all the unpleasantness, appreciative of the patience he offered me. The same qualities that I had once found boring I now saw as comforting, caring, you know what I mean?

"So he and I started to talk again. A cup of coffee here, a dinner together there. As I dealt more honestly with my own feelings, it affected Bud. He too began to reveal more, to express what was inside him. It was as if we had been two different planets, each headed into space on its own particular orbit, doomed to get farther and farther apart from each other. But, then, as my orbit changed, it threw Bud's out of whack too, causing him to plot a new course. The two planets began to move in concert with one another, on more parallel tracks. Before too long, we were headed in similar directions.

"We visited a counselor again, then a minister after that. Both of them helped, though in different ways of course. I think I needed the minister the most. He, a middle-aged man who came to my Mama's church to replace Preacher Babcock six months after she died, walked me through my confusion about God. He told me to accept some mystery, to understand that death is beyond our understanding, that God alone can fathom the 'whys' and 'wherefores' of it all. He reminded me that Christian faith never promised us an absence of pain but that it does give us the promise of enough strength to see us through our pain.

"Somehow, it all began to jell in me. Not that I got all my questions answered. I still don't know why a plane has to crash and snatch the life of a good man away from his wife and kids. I still don't know why one woman gives birth to five kids and another miscarries over and over again. I still don't know a lot of things, big things like that. But the pastor helped me accept the ambiguity of life. Best of all, he helped me see that God ultimately loves me, that God can and does forgive me, that God does give us the strength to endure, to persevere, to win over everything and anything that threatens to defeat us. To say it simply, the Christmas that I forgave Mama, I experienced a spiritual transformation.

"Out of it all, Bud and I moved closer together. Like two streams that had run in separate beds but are brought together in a rushing flood, Bud and I connected, really connected for the first time ever. We canceled the divorce proceedings and, within a year, reconciled with each other. At certain points, of course, the water has churned up again, but over time, we have settled into a common riverbed. Given our newly found love for each other, we've even stirred up a bit of froth from time to time, if you know what I mean.

"Two years after I came home, Bud and I added a third member to our family. No, I didn't get pregnant. The doctor said that with my history of miscarriages I was too old for that and I had to agree. But we did adopt. Our little treasure, a precious black-haired, black-eyed girl, is sitting beside me in her own little rocker right now. She's wearing Christmas red pajamas and is watching me scribble out these words in my journal. (Yes, like Mama, I decided to keep a scrapbook to record the significant events in my life. And, since this tenth anniversary is one of those events, I've been writing on this story for the last week or so.)

"Bud and I don't know exactly when Maleena, an orphan from Romania, was born. So we decided to celebrate her birthday on Christmas Eve each year. By our reckoning, she's about eight now.

"I wonder sometimes if I'm a very good mama for her. But I'm trying, hoping to keep the best qualities of my own mama—her attention to details, her focus on provision, her work to keep the house running smoothly. But I'm also trying to go one step beyond that—to learn from my mama's mistakes. I try every day to tell Maleena how much I love her. I hug her so much I'm sure she gets tired of it. I want to make sure she never doubts how I feel about her.

"With Bud's help, I have the luxury to do this, unlike my mama. Looking back, I now know that Mama did the very best she could with the circumstances life threw at her. She had it tough, a lot tougher than I do. And she became as tough as the circumstances she had to face. Like walking over briers in bare feet. You do it long enough and the feet get calluses or you just can't walk anymore.

"Mama kept walking but it cost her. Put calluses on her soul, covered over most of the tenderness underneath. But the briers weren't her fault. She didn't put them there. So, since the night I found my locket under the tree, I've never felt harsh toward her again. She kept so much to herself, not because she didn't want to share it with me, Colin, and Cory, but because she thought it was too much for us to handle. So, she bottled up all her fears, wedged them deep into her own spirit. She carried the responsibility for all of us—hauled that weight around like a mountain on her own back because she thought it the best way to protect her children.

"In the final analysis, that's all a parent can do, it seems to me—carry out what he or she thinks is best. Sometimes the decisions a parent makes will be right and sometimes they won't. But that's the way life shakes out. Most children never understand this, at least not until they grow up and have children of their own.

"For my part, I came to understand it ten years ago on a frigid Christmas Eve when everything in my life seemed bleak. On that cold night I learned this valuable lesson: in the final analysis, the best any of us can do is this—forgive our parents for the hurts they cause us and bless them for the gifts they leave us. I don't know if that's profound or anything but I do think it's true. At least to me it is.

"Maleena is jumping up and down on the floor beside me.

Bud just reached over and patted me on the arm. And Colin and Cory have just gone to the kitchen to call the rest of the Laws' clan out here to the den. So I guess I'd better stop writing for now. After all, it's Christmas Eve and the fire is blazing and the snow is falling and the family is gathered and it's time to open the gifts."